ONE LAST DANCE

ANNA STONE

© 2019 Anna Stone

All rights reserved. No part of this publication may be replicated, reproduced, or redistributed in any form without the prior written consent of the publisher.

This is a work of fiction. Names, characters, places, and incidents either are the products of the author's imagination or are used fictitiously. Any resemblance to actual persons, living or dead, businesses, companies, events, or locales is entirely coincidental.

Cover by Kasmit Covers

ISBN: 9780648419242

PROLOGUE

ZOE

Zoe took her place on stage for the final act. The curtain rose. Thousands of eyes fixed on her. She took it all in, her pulse thrumming in her ears. She'd stood right here on this stage every night for weeks. That didn't make this moment any less magical.

The stage was hers. The entire concert hall was hers. She held the hearts and minds of every single person in the audience.

But she wasn't dancing for them.

As the orchestra played the opening notes of a gentle melody, Zoe closed her eyes, just for a moment, and took in a breath. Like every other night, she let the stage, the audience, and the bright lights all fade away, until she was back in that empty studio ten years ago, dancing with all her heart for the one person who mattered.

Natasha.

The music rose, and Zoe sprang to life. As she danced, she imagined that it was just the two of them, Zoe performing while Natasha looked on, mesmerized. She imagined Natasha's quiet approval, her rare but radiant smile, her sparkling blue eyes. And her words.

You're so beautiful when you dance for me.

Zoe had treasured those words in her heart for ten years. They rang out in her mind every time she took the stage. She'd never forgotten what it felt like to hear those words from Natasha. At that moment, she'd realized that Natasha, the woman who had haunted her thoughts since the day they'd met, had captured her heart.

Zoe continued dancing for Natasha alone. The ballet was *Giselle*, a tragic otherworldly romance. It was a bittersweet tale of unrequited love, of a beautiful young woman who died of heartbreak. Zoe became Giselle. She felt the high of Giselle's love and the depths of her heartbreak. She channeled all those emotions for Natasha, her teacher.

The music swelled. Zoe leaped into the air, propelled by her partner in a string of jumps, ending in a grand jete. No, she wasn't leaping. She was soaring.

But as Zoe landed, everything was wrong. She was off balance, by the tiniest fraction, but it was enough. As her foot hit the wooden floor, something snapped inside her ankle.

White-hot pain lanced through her foot. She gritted her teeth. *Focus on the music*, Natasha told her. And Zoe did just that, sinking deep into a trance of music, magic, and memories again.

She danced on, striving to reach that impossible perfection she'd been working toward her entire life. To move the audience with the beauty and wonder of her art. To show the world everything Natasha had instilled in her, and the love of dance that the two of them had shared.

The crowd hung onto her every movement, enthralled by Zoe's Giselle. They gasped, laughed, and cried with her. And in the final moments when she, Giselle, returned to her grave at peace, Zoe knew that she had come closer to perfection than ever before.

The show ended with a standing ovation. Zoe curtsied once, and again, and again, until the applause died down and the audience released her. As she left the stage, reality rushed back to her, and the dull ache in her ankle flared hot and bright until it overwhelmed her.

Zoe collapsed onto the floor, her body racked with sobs.

1

ZOE

Zoe lay sprawled across the couch in her older sister's living room. Dawn was rushing from one room to another, packing the last of her things. Zoe had arrived at her sister's house only a week ago, and now Dawn was leaving.

Dawn threw her cell phone charger into her suitcase and turned to study Zoe, her hands on her hips and her brows drawn together. "Are you sure you're going to be okay by yourself?"

Zoe rolled her eyes. Dawn had a tendency to baby her. "I'm twenty-eight. I can take care of myself."

"That's not what I meant. I know you're going through a rough time right now. I don't feel great about leaving you alone."

"I'm okay. Really."

Dawn gave Zoe a skeptical look and zipped up her suitcase.

Zoe stretched out her arms and rearranged herself on the couch. It had been two weeks since her last performance when she'd injured her ankle on stage. Two weeks since she'd been told that she had to stop dancing for the time being if she wanted to avoid serious, permanent damage. Two weeks since Zoe's understudy had replaced her as the star of the Royal London Ballet's production of *Giselle*.

Zoe had been crushed. And suddenly, she'd felt the need to get away from it all. She couldn't stay in London any longer, where her life was nothing but dance. She'd moved to London ten years ago to join the Royal London Ballet. All her friends were dancers, and her days had been filled with classes, training, and rehearsals. She was so deeply immersed in the world of ballet that without it, there was nothing else left for her. The constant reminders that she couldn't be a part of it had been too much to bear.

As soon as she was able to put enough weight on her ankle to walk, Zoe had hopped on a plane and returned to the U.S. to escape the painful reality of being unable to dance. She needed comfort. She needed familiarity. Most of all, she needed a shoulder to cry on.

So, she'd returned to the city she'd called home for most of her life. Her parents had moved away long ago, but her sister, who she'd always been much closer to, remained. Her plan had been to stay with her sister in her apartment for a few weeks so they could spend some time together. But yesterday, Dawn had been called away for work. She was an archeologist, and she often traveled to faraway places where she was completely out of contact for weeks at a time. This time, she was headed to the plains of East Africa.

"Once again, I'm sorry about this," Dawn said. "It really is an emergency."

"It's fine," Zoe replied. "Although I don't get how anything in your line of work can be an emergency."

"Some of what I do is time sensitive. But you don't want to know the details. Whenever I tell you about work stuff, your eyes glaze over."

"Kind of like when I tell you about ballet?"

"Pretty much." Dawn grabbed her phone from the table and slipped it into her purse. "I should get going. I left you a list of things to look after while you're here on the fridge. You're welcome to stay as long as you want. And make yourself at home. What's mine is yours."

"Thanks." Zoe gave her a weak smile.

Dawn sat down next to her. "I wish I could stay, Zoe."

"It's all right. You don't have to worry about me."

"Don't I? For the past week you've done absolutely nothing but lie around watching TV and eating junk food. You've barely left the apartment."

"I'm supposed to be resting my ankle," Zoe said.

"You're supposed to be taking it easy. That means no running around doing pirouettes. It doesn't mean you get to sit around doing nothing."

"Pirouettes? I can barely even do plies."

"Zoe." Dawn placed her hand on Zoe's shoulder. "Promise me you'll take care of yourself while I'm gone."

"I will," Zoe grumbled.

"Zoe." Dawn gave Zoe a stern look. "I'm serious."

"I mean it. I will, I promise."

"Good." Dawn got up and picked up her carry-on bag. She thrust it in Zoe's direction. "Want to help me take my bags downstairs?"

Zoe got up, took the bag from Dawn, and followed her

sister out of the apartment. Her body protested every step of the way, her muscles stiff from disuse. Dawn was right. Zoe had been lying around for too long.

When they reached the street, Dawn pulled her into a hug. "It was good seeing you, even if it was just for a little while. I've missed you so much. With luck, I won't be away too long this time."

"It's okay," Zoe said. "Have fun."

"I will. And don't lose hope. Everything will be okay in the end."

After reminding Zoe to water her plants, Dawn hailed a passing cab and hopped into it.

Zoe headed back up to Dawn's apartment. It seemed so empty. She gazed absently around the living room. What was she supposed to do with herself? Not just right now, but with the rest of her life? She was getting old, at least for a ballet dancer. Her body wasn't what it used to be. Even before her injury, retirement had been looming.

And now, her career was as good as over.

But Zoe was born to dance. She'd lived and breathed ballet since she was six. She didn't know anything else. Without dance, she had nothing.

Zoe sighed. Dawn was right. She had to stop moping. She'd always been prone to letting her emotions run away with her. And she always focused on the worst-case scenario. Technically, she was only on leave. Her physical therapist had said that it was too early to give her a timeline for her recovery. If she could get back on her feet soon, there was a possibility that she'd be able to return to dance for the Royal London Ballet in their next production.

It was a small chance. But it was something.

Zoe put her hands on her hips. No more feeling sorry for herself. No more sitting around in sweatpants. She couldn't afford to get out of shape. Which also meant no more takeout and junk food.

Zoe headed into the kitchen and opened Dawn's pantry. The shelves were practically bare. If she wanted to cook a healthy dinner, she'd have to go shopping.

Zoe entered the grocery store, her ankle throbbing faintly from the short walk from her apartment. She was supposed to be walking on it, but she hadn't been keeping up with the exercises her physical therapist had assigned her. She made a mental note to start doing them again.

She headed down an aisle at random, a basket in her hand. Zoe was sure she looked like a mess. She'd thrown a coat she'd borrowed from her much larger sister over the old yoga pants and t-shirt she'd been lounging around in all day, and her hair was in disarray.

She hoped no one would recognize her. Outside of the ballet world, being a principal dancer meant nothing, so she wasn't exactly a celebrity. However, her occasional appearances in mainstream magazines and TV meant she had some degree of fame. Back in London, she'd get stopped on the streets by a fan a few times a week. So far, she'd managed to fly under the radar back here in the States. But then again, she'd barely left her sister's apartment.

As she walked past a freezer filled with ice cream, she was hit with an unmistakable craving. She stopped. Maybe a little junk food wouldn't hurt. Zoe scanned the tubs of ice cream in the freezer. *Mint choc chip, or rocky road?* For some reason, it seemed like the most difficult decision ever.

She sighed. Just a few weeks ago, she'd been on center stage, dancing her heart out, on top of the world. Now, she was at the grocery store in faded yoga pants, unable to make a simple choice.

Screw it. Zoe grabbed a pint in each flavor, then wandered over to the produce aisle. She surveyed the fresh food before her. She was pretty sure she'd forgotten what vegetables tasted like. As she reached for a bunch of something that resembled lettuce, a woman slid up next to her, a shopping basket slung over her arm.

Zoe glanced in her direction. Her heart stopped.

Natasha?

The woman's head was down, so Zoe couldn't see her face, but everything about her was familiar. The way she held herself, with the poise of a seasoned dancer, even though she'd stopped dancing long before Zoe had met her. Her long brown hair, which fell loosely over her shoulders. Her seemingly delicate frame, which was hidden under a long black coat.

Zoe's pulse began to race. It hadn't occurred to her that she might run into her former ballet teacher while here in the city. Zoe didn't even know Natasha still lived here. She never thought she'd see Natasha again. The two of them hadn't spoken since that night ten years ago.

And that night, Zoe had left in tears.

Zoe didn't harbor any bad feelings toward Natasha. Everything between them had been complicated, and it had all remained unspoken until it was too late. Still, seeing Natasha brought up all the conflict and turmoil of that night. Not to mention all the other feelings Zoe still had for her. She still felt that irresistible pull of desire. And they hadn't even spoken a word to each other yet.

Natasha turned toward Zoe slightly, reaching toward her to grab a head of lettuce. It was unmistakable now. This was Natasha. *Her* Natasha. She had the same stormy blue-gray eyes that spoke more than her words ever did. The same face, so smooth and defined that looked like it had been carved from marble. The same flawless skin, pale everywhere except for the faint tinge of pink on her cheeks.

"Natasha," Zoe said softly.

Natasha looked up at the sound of her name. Her eyes met Zoe's. All the air left Zoe's lungs.

Recognition dawned on Natasha's face. "Zoe?"

What was she supposed to say to Natasha? To the woman who had tormented her mind for ten long years? To the woman she thought about every time she stepped on stage?

To the woman who had been the subject of her fantasies for far longer than she cared to admit?

"It's really you," Natasha said. "What are you doing here? I thought you were in London."

"I'm on leave." It was all Zoe could think of to say.

"Right. I heard about your injury. I'm sorry."

"You did?"

"You know how it is," Natasha said. "The ballet world is small. News gets around."

"Oh." A small part of Zoe had hoped Natasha had been keeping track of her.

Silence lingered between them. Over the years, Zoe had

thought of a million things she wished she'd been able to say to Natasha. But now, she couldn't think of anything.

"I see you haven't changed," Natasha said.

Zoe frowned. "What do you mean?"

Natasha pointed to the ice cream in Zoe's basket.

"Oh. I'm just picking up some things for dinner. I got a little sidetracked." Zoe grabbed some lettuce and added it to her basket. "See? Vegetables."

"Right."

Zoe's cheeks burned. *See? Vegetables?* Apparently being in Natasha's presence had turned her back into that awkward eighteen-year-old, blinded by her desire for a woman she shouldn't have desired at all. She combed her fingers through her hair, cursing herself for leaving the apartment looking like this.

Natasha grabbed a couple of tomatoes and placed them into her basket. "I'll let you get back to it. I have to head back to work."

"Are you still teaching?" Zoe asked.

"Yes. Still at the Academy."

They both stood there, neither saying a word. Zoe's brain was screaming something at her, but she couldn't quite work out what it was. She was lost in a fog of Natasha.

"It was nice running into you," Natasha said.

"Yeah," Zoe replied. "Same to you."

Natasha gave her a polite nod and headed toward the front of the store.

Zoe stood rooted in place, unable to move. It had been ten years, yet Natasha still had the power to unravel her with just a look, to send Zoe's mind racing with memories of her, to make her heart and body ache with need.

Then why was she letting Natasha walk out of her life again?

Zoe dropped her basket and hurried to the front of the store. The checkouts were empty. Her stomach sank. Had Natasha already left? She couldn't have gone far. Zoe rushed through the checkout, pulled the door to the store open—

—and nearly ran head-first into Natasha.

"Zoe." Natasha brought her hand up to her chest in surprise.

"Have dinner with me," Zoe blurted out. "Tonight. At my place. It's not mine, it's my sister's. But she's away, and—" She took a breath, gathering her thoughts. "I could use the company."

Natasha didn't respond at first. Zoe couldn't read her expression. Was she trying to figure out whether Zoe had just asked her on a date? *Had* Zoe just asked her on a date? She didn't even know herself.

"All right," Natasha said. "I'll give you my number and you can send me your address."

The two of them quickly exchanged phone numbers, and Natasha said goodbye again.

Zoe watched her disappear onto the street. *Wow.* What were the chances of the two of them running into each other, the first time Zoe had ventured out into the city since she'd gotten here? It was lucky. Really lucky.

Or maybe it was fate.

2
NATASHA

Natasha still remembered her first lesson with Zoe.

She and Zoe had crossed paths before at the exclusive ballet academy where Natasha taught, but they'd never spoken a word to each other. Natasha had watched Zoe dance in the school's productions and recitals over the years, but Zoe had been just been one of many students, and Natasha hadn't remembered much about her. Apparently, when it came to talent, Zoe was one of the best dancers at the academy. But in other areas, she was lacking.

Natasha's job was to fix that. Zoe was the first private student she'd been assigned. All the senior students at the academy took both solo and group classes. Most of the teachers taught both. However, because of her inexperience compared to her colleagues, Natasha had only taught group classes with the younger kids. Half the time she felt like she was babysitting. Since she was one of the most junior instructors at the academy, she was at the bottom of the ladder.

But she was good at her job. And one of her colleagues, Luc, had finally noticed. He was retiring, so he'd assigned the students he taught privately to the rest of the teachers. He personally asked Natasha to take Zoe on. Natasha said yes immediately. She was looking forward to getting to teach someone as advanced as Zoe.

At least, she *had* been. It was time for their lesson to start, and Zoe was nowhere to be found.

Zoe should have come to class early to prepare. Any serious dancer would have been. It was almost insulting. This was no local dance studio. This was the National Ballet Academy, one of the best ballet schools in the country. Only the most talented dancers gained admission. Most of the school's graduates went on to get jobs with major ballet companies. Zoe should have been one of those students. At eighteen, she was at the age most serious dancers received job offers through auditions or being scouted at competitions.

Several more minutes passed. Just when Natasha was about to give up, the door to the studio swung open. Zoe entered the room, a bag over her shoulder, hastily tying a thin scarf around her head to hold back the curls that had escaped from her bun.

Natasha put her hands on her hips. "You're late." It was only by a few minutes. But she expected better from someone who was serious about ballet.

"I know, I know." Zoe dropped her bag and finished tying up her hair. "Sorry."

Natalie looked her up and down. She wore a black leotard and tights, with a short blue wrap skirt tied around her waist and a leg warmer on one ankle.

"So," Zoe said. "Are we going to start?"

"Yes," Natasha replied. "Right after you warm up."

"I don't need to. I just had a group class."

"That doesn't matter. Go warm up."

For a moment, Natasha thought Zoe was going to roll her eyes. Instead, she walked over to the barre and began a series of stretches.

Natasha examined her student. Zoe had the ideal body for ballet. She was short and lithe, with long, willowy legs and a swan-like neck. Her small frame hid powerful muscles. As Zoe pulled one leg behind her, her toes pointed upward, the arch of her foot curved in a way that was perfect for dancing en pointe. She had the flexibility too. As shallow as it was, having the 'right' body was everything in ballet. Zoe had the body. She had the talent.

What was missing?

Zoe looked up in the mirror, her large brown eyes meeting Natasha's.

Natasha folded her arms across her chest. "Next time, I expect you to be warmed up before I arrive. Which means coming in early. We only get a few lessons a week together. I don't want to waste time waiting for you to stretch."

"Luc liked to start the lesson with stretches," Zoe said. "So we could take the time to talk about anything I wanted to work on."

"I'm not Luc. If you want to discuss something, you can come early," Natasha added.

"Okay."

Natasha had spoken to Luc about Zoe. Apparently, Zoe's performance was unpredictable, and she tended to do badly during competitions and auditions. He'd said that what Zoe really needed was a coach. Someone who would keep her focused. It seemed like he was hoping Natasha's cool-headedness would rub off on Zoe.

But Natasha couldn't help but wonder if Luc had just wanted to palm off this undisciplined student to someone desperate enough to take her. Either way, Natasha had her work cut out for her.

After a couple of minutes, Zoe straightened up. "I'm all done."

Zoe was *not* done. Her stretches had been hurried and half-hearted. But Natasha didn't press the point. If she was going to work with someone like Zoe, both of them were going to have to make concessions.

"Let's start with barre work," Natasha said.

"Do we have to?" Zoe asked. "I already did it in my class earlier."

"Yes. There's a reason lessons proceed in the order they do. We start with simple, foundational movements to get the body warmed up before proceeding to more strenuous work."

"I know. I've been taking ballet classes since I was six. But Luc usually skipped barre work if I had a group class beforehand."

"Once again, I'm not Luc. There's a proper way to do things." As much as she'd looked up to her now-retired colleague, he had unconventional methods. Clearly, they hadn't worked on Zoe. "Besides, it will help me get an idea of how you move."

"Can I show you something else then?" Zoe asked. "Something more involved?"

Natasha hesitated. Maybe it was a good idea to let Zoe

have a say in their lessons. She wasn't one of Natasha's ten-year-olds, after all. Besides, seeing Zoe dance up close would give Natasha a good idea of what she was capable of.

"Fine," Natasha said. "You have a solo in the academy's upcoming production of *A Midsummer Night's Dream*. Why don't you show me that?"

A smile grew on Zoe's face. "Sure."

"I'll cue the music."

Zoe got into position. Natasha walked over to the stereo system in the corner. Unlike in group classes, they didn't have the luxury of a live pianist, so they had to make do with CDs played over the studio's sound system. Natasha found the CD she was looking for, slid it into the stereo, and pressed play. When the music began, Zoe started to dance.

Natasha's mouth almost dropped open. At once, it was like Zoe had undergone a transformation, from surly student to seasoned ballet dancer. Her technique was as flawless as any professional's. But that wasn't what stood out to Natasha. Zoe possessed an unrestrained grace that had her captivated. She could feel the passion radiating from the young dancer. Ballet was an art form. It was about expression, telling a story using nothing but the body. And the story Zoe told was beautiful.

Natasha watched her carefully, scrutinizing her movements. The solo was a challenging one, fast-paced and technically complex, but Zoe took the movements and made the dance hers. She performed it effortlessly, becoming the embodiment of *ballon*, that impossible illusion of lightness that ballet dancers strove for.

As Zoe performed a perfect triple pirouette, Natasha

was reminded of a certain other dancer she knew so well. *Paige.* While Paige was much more refined, Zoe was freer, but her style had that same magnetic quality that made it impossible for Natasha to tear her eyes away.

It was undeniable. Zoe belonged on center stage.

But as the song drew on, mistakes began to slip through. Tiny errors, faltering form, Zoe's sprite-like lightness replaced by a weight in each step. It wasn't noticeable to the untrained eye, but Natasha could see it. It was like the Zoe she'd been watching moments ago had been replaced by someone else entirely.

Natasha paused the music. "Stop."

Zoe froze in place. "Is something wrong?"

"What happened just now?"

"What do you mean?"

"The first half was good. Then everything fell apart. Why?"

Zoe shrugged. "I don't know."

"Did you get tired?" Natasha asked. If stamina was the issue, they could work on that.

"No."

"Were you distracted?"

"No."

Natasha studied Zoe with a frown. "Luc says you've gone to plenty of auditions this year but haven't gotten any offers from companies yet. Do you have any idea why?"

"Not really."

"Do you get nervous?"

Zoe just shrugged again.

Natasha wanted to groan. Were shrugs and one-word answers all she was going to get from her student? Zoe was an adult, not some sullen teenager. But if she was going to behave like one of Natasha's younger students, than Natasha would have to treat her like one.

"Let's go back to basics. We'll start with barre work."

Zoe took her place at the barre without complaint. But the sour look on her face had returned.

Natasha held back a sigh and turned on the music. "First position."

3

NATASHA

Natasha headed up to Zoe's apartment. She'd been surprised to run into Zoe after so long. She'd been even more surprised by Zoe's dinner invitation. When they'd parted ways ten years ago, they hadn't been on good terms—or so Natasha had thought. It had been her fault entirely. Had Zoe forgiven her?

Natasha reached Zoe's apartment and knocked on the door.

"Just a minute," Zoe yelled from inside.

Natasha stood and waited, a bottle of wine in her hands. She had no idea if Zoe even liked wine, but she hadn't wanted to show up empty-handed to whatever this dinner was. Just a catch-up dinner between two friends who had fallen out of touch years ago? No, they'd never been friends. They'd never been just teacher and student either. They'd been so much more.

A fact which Natasha had never let herself admit until it was too late.

She knew all too well that she couldn't undo the past.

Natasha carried with her a lifetime of regrets, and everything that had happened with Zoe back then was one of them. So much time had passed since then. And they weren't teacher and student any longer.

Could they pick up where they left off?

It wasn't a good idea. Zoe was only in the city temporarily. Sooner or later, she'd go back to London. There was no point in even entertaining the idea of anything happening between them.

Zoe opened the door. Her hair was tied up in a ponytail, and she wore a striped scarf wrapped around her head to hold back the curls that had sprung free. That was just about the only part of her appearance that was unchanged. In the past, Zoe had never worn makeup, except for the heavy, stage-ready looks she'd sported for performances. Now, her wide brown eyes were ringed in a smoky gray, and her dark bronze cheeks shimmered. She wore a long, flowy blouse and black jeans that elongated her slim frame.

Zoe had always been beautiful. Natasha had never allowed herself to appreciate it. But as Zoe stood before her, with a vibrant smile and enchanting eyes, it was impossible not to see it. And it was impossible not to feel the sparks that leaped between them.

"Natasha," Zoe said. "Your timing is perfect. I just finished making dinner."

"Great." Natasha held out the bottle. "I hope you like wine."

"I do. Thanks."

Natasha followed Zoe into the apartment. It was immediately obvious that the space wasn't Zoe's. Everything was neat and carefully organized, the scattering of plants the only sign that the house was lived in. Apparently, Zoe and her sister were very different people.

Zoe led Natasha to the dining table. "Have a seat. I'll open the wine."

Natasha sat down while Zoe went back and forth between the kitchen, bringing out several piping hot dishes, waving away Natasha's offer to help. Finally, the sound of a cork popping came from the kitchen. A moment later, Zoe joined her at the table.

"This is impressive." Natasha gestured toward the food. "And it's enough to feed an army."

"Yeah, I kind of went overboard." Zoe poured them each a glass. "Dig in."

Natasha helped herself to the nearest dish. "How long have you been back?"

"Just a week. I wanted to get away from it all. Take some time to rest and recuperate. Plus, it was hard being surrounded by ballet and other dancers and not being able to dance myself."

"I can imagine," Natasha said. "I know how rough injuries can be on dancers. It's hard to stop and rest when you're used to pushing through everything."

"Yeah. I thought getting away would help, but instead, I've just ended up sitting around moping." Zoe winced. "Sorry, I don't mean to be a downer."

"No, it's fine."

They continued to eat. There was a hint of tension lingering over them. Was that because of the way they had last parted ways, or something else? Was now a good time to clear the air?

"I still can't believe I ran into you today," Zoe said. "In a city this big, what are the chances?"

"The odds are pretty low," Natasha replied. "It was a happy coincidence."

"Yeah. God, how long has it been?"

"Ten years." Not that Natasha had been counting. "So, what have you been up to all this time?"

"Well, I've stayed with the Royal London Ballet. I worked my way up to principal dancer within two years of joining the company. I was pretty surprised. I wasn't expecting it to happen so fast." Zoe's eyes grew distant. "I'll never forget my first performance as principal."

"Swan Lake," Natasha said. "It's always been one of my favorites. The technical complexity is impressive."

"It was the hardest role I've ever danced. It's one of my favorites now too." Zoe paused. "How did you know my debut as a principal dancer was Swan Lake?"

"I've been following your career over the years."

"Really?"

"All the teachers at the academy like to keep track of former students. But I admit, I took a more personal interest in what you were up to." Natasha had almost gotten on a plane to London to see Zoe's debut. And it hadn't been the last time she'd thought about going to watch her former student perform.

Zoe glanced down at her plate shyly. "What about you? What have you been doing all this time?"

"Not much has changed for me. As you know, I'm still teaching at the academy. I'm one of the senior instructors now. No more babysitting the ten-year-olds."

"That's great. You must be pretty happy about that."

"I am," Natasha said. "I've taught lots of talented students over the years who have gone on to do great things. Of course, none of them were anywhere near as talented as you."

"And outside of work? How are things? Are you seeing anyone?"

Natasha hid a smile. Zoe didn't have a subtle bone in her body. "Not at the moment. I've had relationships, of course. But there hasn't been anyone special. Honestly, it's been years since I've been in anything serious." Natasha hadn't intended to share that much. Zoe had that effect on her. They were slipping back into old habits already. "How about you? Is there a lucky woman in your life?"

"Definitely not. I've had my fair share of flings, but anything long term was too difficult because of my job. It's so demanding. You'd have to be crazy to date a professional ballet dancer." Zoe cringed. "Sorry, I didn't mean—"

"It's fine. I agree with you." Natasha had learned that the hard way. She picked up the bottle of wine and refilled both their glasses. "Weren't you seeing that concert pianist at one point?"

"Ellen. How do you know about her?"

"Are you kidding? That article about the two of you made a big splash. A ballet superstar and a piano prodigy dating? And it's not every day a principal dancer in one of the major ballet companies comes out. Not a female one anyway. Everyone heard about it."

"Right. I forgot all about that. Honestly, I just wanted to put the rumors about me to rest."

"It must have been a huge weight off your shoulders," Natasha said.

"It was. Ellen and I didn't last very long after that, though. We weren't very good together in the first place."

The evening wore on. Natasha and Zoe chatted away, the food on their plates slowly growing cold. By the time they finished dinner, they'd reached the end of the bottle of wine.

"More wine?" Zoe asked. "My sister has a pretty big collection."

"Does she know that you're drinking her wine?" Natasha asked.

Zoe shrugged. "I'll replace it before she gets back."

"Why not, then?" Natasha could think of a dozen reasons why not. She'd already had several glasses. She was feeling a little too relaxed. And she was starting to remember why she and Zoe had gotten so close in the first place.

"Why don't you have a seat on the couch?" Zoe said.

Natasha wandered over to the couch, watching as Zoe walked over to the wine rack in the corner. Naturally, she moved with the grace of a dancer, and the confidence of someone who had spent a lifetime on stage. In the past, Zoe's confidence had fluctuated wildly depending on her mood. But now, she had a self-assuredness that Natasha found so irresistible.

Zoe joined Natasha by the couch, another bottle of red wine in her hand. She poured them both a generous glass and sat down. "Why are you looking at me like that?"

"No reason." Natasha sat back and crossed her legs. "I just can't believe how far you've come. Look at you. Look at all you've achieved."

"Yeah. I guess I have come a long way." Zoe sighed. "But it's all over now."

"Why do you say that? Isn't this break only temporary?"

"Technically, it is. But I don't know how long I'll be out of action. Chances are, by the time I'm done reconditioning my body, it'll be too late for me to join the next production. It'll be hard for me to come back after that. And honestly, even if I hadn't been injured, I probably would have been replaced as a principal in the next year or two. I'm getting old in ballet terms. My career is as good as over."

"Maybe not," Natasha said. "There are other options. Lots of dancers go on to be choreographers or artistic directors. Even teachers."

Zoe raised an eyebrow. "Me? Teaching?"

"Why not?"

"I'm not exactly the strict type."

"Who says you need to be? Not all teachers are strict."

"Maybe not compared to you," Zoe muttered.

"I wasn't that bad," Natasha said.

"I didn't say there was anything wrong with being strict." Zoe smiled. "It was exactly what I needed."

"Well, it seems to have worked."

"Yes, it did." Zoe took a sip of her wine. "So, you said before that you haven't had a student as talented as me yet. Does that mean I'm still your favorite?"

Natasha looked her up and down. "You haven't changed at all, have you?"

"Nope. You didn't answer my question."

"Well, let's just say, I've never had a student quite like you."

"Is that a good thing?" Zoe asked.

"Mostly. I haven't forgotten how much you used to get under my skin in those first few weeks."

"You got under my skin too. But not in a bad way."

Natasha scoffed. "I'm pretty sure you hated me at first."

"Okay, maybe I did a little," Zoe said. "But that changed pretty quickly. You still frustrated me, but for entirely different reasons."

Zoe's smooth voice sent a shiver up Natasha's neck. "I take it back," she said. "You have changed. You were nowhere near this bold back then."

"Maybe I was, and you never noticed." Zoe peered at Natasha through long lashes. "Did it ever occur to you that my sloppy alignment was just to give you an excuse to 'correct' me by touching me?"

"I don't believe you. You were much too serious about your ballet career to do something like that."

"Was I?"

"You were! Even you wouldn't go that far."

"Okay, you caught me," Zoe said. "I never did screw up on purpose. But I considered it so many times."

Natasha shook her head. She was the same old Zoe in so many ways, yet in others, she was completely different. "This confidence of yours. It suits you. I suppose being the darling of the ballet world will do that to you."

"I didn't get there on my own. I had lots of help. And I'll always be grateful for that."

Natasha swirled her wine around in the glass as silence fell over them. The couch was on the small side, and they were sitting close to each other. The scent of Zoe's skin took her back to their lessons together. It was sweet and earthy, but now it didn't have that hint of sweat from dancing for hours on end. It triggered something inside

Natasha, that magnetic attraction that she'd always tried to suppress.

"I'm so glad we ran into each other," Zoe said. "I've thought about you a lot over the years."

"I've thought about you too," Natasha replied.

"Have you ever wondered what would have happened if things had been different? If I hadn't moved away? If I hadn't been your student? If the timing had been better?"

"I try not to dwell on the past." It was true. Natasha tried her hardest. But she'd never been good at moving on.

"Oh."

Natasha cursed herself silently. She should have known better than to speak so dismissively. She set down her glass and placed her hand on the other woman's thigh. "I never wondered what would have been. But I wondered what would happen if we ever reconnected. I thought of getting in touch through the years. But so much time had passed. And there was so much distance between us." She didn't just mean the fact that they were on opposite sides of the world.

"Yeah. But that's not the case anymore, is it?" Zoe slid her hand to cover Natasha's. "We're both right here. And there's nothing standing between us."

"That's right," Natasha said, the embers of desire within her igniting. With little more than a touch, Zoe had turned her world upside down once again.

Zoe leaned in closer, gazing at Natasha with those wide brown eyes of hers. There was the faint scent of wine on Zoe's lips. They were perfect lips, so full and pink. Had they always looked so inviting?

"I've been waiting so long to do this," Zoe whispered.

Their lips crashed together in a firm, ravenous kiss. A thrill went through Natasha's body. They had kissed once before, but that had been sweet and fleeting, almost an accident. This was no accident. Natasha could feel the intent in Zoe's lips, an urgency that made Natasha want to devour her.

Zoe's fingers tightened around Natasha's hand. Natasha's free hand crept up the side of Zoe's neck to caress her cheek, tracing the curve of Zoe's cheekbone with her thumb. Zoe let out a murmur and grabbed Natasha's waist, urging her closer. Their bodies pressed together, sending a wave of heat over Natasha's skin—

Natasha froze. All of a sudden, everything she had felt for Zoe back then had come rushing back at her. All the passion, the turmoil, the indecision.

The guilt.

Zoe drew back, searching Natasha's eyes. "Is everything okay?"

"Yes," Natasha said. "It's just that, this isn't a good idea, you and me. I mean, you're only in the city temporarily and all." It was a weak excuse. But she didn't know how to explain what she was feeling. She hadn't even figured it out herself.

"Right. Yeah, I get it."

The disappointment and confusion were clear in Zoe's voice. It wasn't surprising. Natasha had been sending Zoe signals all night. But she shouldn't have kissed her. She should have known better.

"I'm sorry." She glanced toward the door. "It's getting late. I should go."

"Oh," Zoe said. "Okay."

Natasha got up and gathered her things. "Thank you. For dinner."

"No problem," Zoe said. "Thanks for the wine."

Zoe led her to the door. Well, more like, Zoe followed her, because Natasha suddenly had to get out of there as fast as she could. She slipped on her coat, fumbling with the buttons.

"I'll be around for another week or two at least," Zoe said. "In case you wanted to…"

"Right." Natasha finished buttoning her coat. "I'll let you know. Thanks again for dinner."

Without waiting for a reply, Natasha left the apartment.

4
ZOE

*Z*oe hated Natasha.

At least, she had for the first few weeks of classes with her. It had been the same every lesson. Natasha would spend most of that time telling Zoe to focus. Zoe would grit her teeth and try her hardest. They'd both get frustrated. And they would get absolutely nowhere.

Zoe doubted today's lesson would be any different. And she was *not* in the mood to deal with Natasha's nagging.

Standing before the mirror in the bathroom at the academy, Zoe splashed some water onto her face and dried it off with a paper towel. She was late already, but she didn't care. She'd had the worst day. She was upset. She was angry. She was frustrated. And she was struggling to keep all those feelings from boiling over.

It didn't help that her older sister had just left for some archeological dig in Brazil as part of her grad program. She was completely out of contact. Dawn wasn't just Zoe's sister. She was her best friend. Zoe missed her, now more than ever. She desperately wished she could talk to Dawn about everything that was going on.

The door to the bathroom opened. Two girls from Zoe's ballet class walked in, wearing matching pink leotards, chatting animatedly. They spotted Zoe, then started speaking to each other in hushed whispers.

Zoe ignored them. She wasn't going to let them get to her. Well, it was too late for that. But she wasn't going to let them see that they were getting to her. Keeping as calm as she could, she slung her bag over her shoulder and left the bathroom, heading for the studio for her lesson with Natasha.

As soon as she walked through the door, she was met by Natasha's icy glare.

"You're late." Natasha didn't even give her a chance to make an excuse. "Start stretching."

Zoe said nothing. She dumped her bag and went over to the barre and stretched. As usual, Natasha glowered at her while she did. Zoe resisted the urge to glower back. She was trying her hardest to get along with Natasha, but it was impossible. They were complete opposites. Natasha was so serious and strict. She was more like a drill sergeant than a dance teacher.

Zoe had no idea why her old teacher had assigned her to Natasha. Luc had been one of the best teachers at the academy. He used to dance for the New York Ballet. He'd been teaching her since she started at the school six years ago. Zoe had always enjoyed his lessons. But now, she was stuck with this no-name instructor who bossed her around like she was a kid.

Zoe straightened up. "I'm done."

"Let's get started," Natasha said.

Zoe took her place for yet more barre work. Ballet lessons always followed the same structure, and Natasha always insisted on going through every single component of them for the sake of doing things 'the proper way.' It didn't make sense. Zoe got enough of basics in group classes. She was wasting her time doing plies over and over when she could be working on more advanced exercises.

And time was something Zoe couldn't afford to waste. She was almost nineteen now. She needed to get a position with a company soon, or it would all be over for her. Everything she'd worked for since she was six would be for nothing. Her dreams would be dashed.

Natasha listed a series of steps and started the music. Zoe tried her hardest to follow Natasha's relentless barrage of instructions. But it was hard enough on a good day, let alone a day like this. Zoe was off her game.

"Don't drop your elbow." Natasha reached out and pushed on Zoe's elbow in. "This is where you should be. Again."

Zoe got into second position and repeated the movements for what had to be the hundredth time.

"Look at where your left arm is. Do it again, and think about what you're doing."

Zoe went through the exercise again.

"No," Natasha said. "Stop."

"What is it this time?"

"You're not finishing your movements. You're taking shortcuts."

Zoe gritted her teeth. "I'm trying."

"Are you?" Natasha asked, her voice rising. "Because it

doesn't look like you're trying. You show up late, again, and everything you're doing is sloppy and unfocused! Do you even want to be here?"

"Of course I do."

"Then why aren't you acting like it?"

Zoe's insides began to boil. "I'm trying, okay? Stop hounding me!"

Natasha's head flinched back. Zoe braced herself, waiting for Natasha's wrath.

Instead, Natasha held up her hands. "You're right. I'm sorry, I shouldn't have said that. And I shouldn't have snapped at you."

Zoe said nothing. She didn't know how to react.

"Is something wrong?" Natasha asked. "You seem distracted."

"I'm fine." Zoe's head was cooling down now. "I've just had a rough day, that's all."

"Do you want to talk about it?"

"No." Natasha was the last person Zoe wanted to discuss these problems with.

"Look, I know we don't get along very well, but as your teacher, your well-being is my concern. If there's something going on, I want to know about it. You can trust me."

"It's not something you'd understand."

"You'd be surprised," Natasha said. "Try me."

"Well, it's not like you're not going to hear about it anyway," Zoe said. "It's all anyone is talking about. I'm surprised you haven't heard already."

"Heard what?"

"The rumors. About me."

Natasha's brows drew together. "If there's something

going on, you need to tell me. The academy won't tolerate bullying and spreading rumors."

"Is it really bullying if it's true?" Zoe asked.

"Zoe, just tell me what's going on."

"I don't know how it started, but there are all these rumors going around that I'm a lesbian. And now half the girls I have classes with won't talk to me or go near me. It's like we're in middle school again."

Natasha crossed her arms. "I'm going to put a stop to this. I'll talk to the director."

"That will just make it worse!"

"I have to do something. Clearly, this harassment is affecting you."

"That's not what's getting to me," Zoe said. "Sure, it hurts. But I can handle it. I've spent my whole life putting up with bullies and being an outsider. What bothers me is that in this day and age, people still think that being attracted to someone of the same gender is wrong and shameful."

"So, what they're saying is true?"

"Yes, it's true! It's just another thing that makes me different from everyone else." Zoe balled her hands into fists. "I learned a long time ago that the only way I could be happy was to embrace my differences. But it's just so hard to do that sometimes!"

Zoe fell silent. Natasha had tensed up, an uneasy look in her eyes. *Great. Now she probably thinks I'm a freak like everyone else does.*

Natasha squeezed Zoe's shoulder. "I'm sorry you're going through this. I know how hard this must be for you."

"No, you don't," Zoe said.

Natasha broke away and sat down on the bench behind them. "Sit down with me."

Zoe sat down, fidgeting with her fingers in her lap.

"I'm going to tell you something not many people know about me," Natasha said. "When I was even younger than you, I fell in love with another girl. We started dating in secret, but we still had to deal with all kinds of awful rumors and gossip. It was tough."

Zoe's mouth fell open slightly. "Really? You're... I didn't know."

"I don't make a habit of broadcasting my sexuality. That girl I fell in love with, we ended up staying together for more than ten years. We only broke up recently, but when we were together, we kept it a secret the entire time. She had a high-profile job where being out would have caused problems. And I kept it under wraps for the sake of my career too. People don't like the idea of people like me teaching their kids."

"But, isn't it hard?" Zoe asked. "Keeping it a secret? Isn't it lonely?"

Natasha nodded. "Sometimes."

"It's 2009. This kind of thing shouldn't matter anymore. It isn't fair."

"I know. But the world is changing. One day it won't matter."

"I hope you're right," Zoe said.

"I am. It might seem impossible when you're eighteen, but things change. Now, are you sure you don't want me to say something to the director?"

"I'm sure."

"Just remember, the academy isn't the whole world,"

Natasha touched Zoe's arm reassuringly. Goosebumps spread along Zoe skin. "I know it's your world right now, but it's not the real world. You're surrounded by a bunch of driven, hyper-competitive teenagers. It's a breeding ground for all kinds of nastiness. Things get better once you leave all this high-school crap behind."

"I hope so," Zoe mumbled.

"And if you ever need to talk, I'm here."

"Thanks, Natasha." Zoe sighed. "Can we keep going with the lesson?"

"Sure."

As Zoe returned to the barre, her stomach fluttered. She pushed the feeling down deeper. So she and Natasha had something in common. It didn't mean they were going to be friends.

But maybe Natasha wasn't as bad as Zoe thought she was.

5
ZOE

Zoe sat on the bed in her old physical therapist's office. She'd tracked him down when she'd returned home. Theo had been her physical therapist since she started dancing, so he was happy to squeeze her in. They'd spent the last half hour going through a battery of tests. Zoe's ankle throbbed.

Theo grabbed Zoe's heel and twisted her foot gently. "Does this hurt?"

"No," Zoe said.

"Then why are you wincing?"

"Fine. Yes, it hurts. But only a little."

"What about this?" He twisted her foot in the other direction.

Pain shot up through Zoe's ankle. She bit the inside of her cheek. "It's fine."

"Zoe." Theo crossed his arms. "You know I can't help you if you're not honest with me."

"I know," Zoe said. "But I really want to get back out

there. I know I won't be dancing en pointe anytime soon, but I want to do something more intense than yoga."

"I know how you feel. I've treated enough ballet dancers to know how hard it is to rest when you're used to pushing through your injuries."

It wasn't like ballet dancers had any choice but to power through their injuries. Zoe knew that all too well. Pain had been a normal part of her life since she started dancing. She'd had sprains, tendonitis, broken toes. There were parts of her body that hurt from old injuries every time she danced. But she just gritted her teeth and kept going every time.

"This is one injury you just can't push through," Theo said. "You need to rest your ankle."

"For how long?" Zoe asked.

Theo pulled up a chair and sat down across from her. "It's hard to say, exactly. You did a lot of damage when you kept dancing on that injured ankle."

It wasn't like Zoe could have just stopped. It was right in the middle of the performance. The whole show would have ground to a halt. And it hadn't even occurred to her to stop. She'd been in the zone, running on pure adrenaline and endorphins like she always did when she was on stage. She'd danced through the pain without thinking.

And now she was paying the price.

"Just tell me," Zoe said. "How long before I can dance again?"

"My recommendation is that you don't perform any strenuous physical activity for three months."

Zoe's heart sank. "Three months? But that's too long." She wouldn't be able to recondition her body and get into shape by the time rehearsals for the next production started. She would miss out entirely.

And that would mean the end of her career.

"I know it sounds like a long time," Theo said. "But rushing back into things will only make it worse. Even after the three months are over, it will take a while for your ankle to return to full strength."

That was it. It was over for her. A part of her had known it was coming from the moment she'd left the stage that night. The hope that everything would work out was the only thing that had kept her going. But now, all hope was lost.

"I'm sorry, Zoe," Theo said.

"It's okay." Zoe got up from the bed and slipped her shoe back on.

"I'll email you those extra exercises. They'll help with the healing process."

Zoe nodded. But there was no point in doing them. Not if she was never going to be able to dance again.

While walking home from Theo's office, Zoe got a message from Dawn, saying she'd give Zoe a call in half an hour. She rushed home and settled on her sister's couch with her phone next to her.

A few minutes later, it began to ring. Zoe picked up the call, her sister's face appearing on the screen.

"Hey Zo," Dawn said.

"Hi Dawn," Zoe replied. "How's Tanzania?"

"Hot and wet. My hair is going crazy. It sounds like

we're going to be here for at least a few weeks, so I have a lot more of this weather to look forward to."

"Sounds like fun."

Dawn peered over her shoulder. "I only have ten minutes before we leave town. This is the last time I'll be able to talk to you for a while, so I thought I'd check how things are going."

"Everything is fine. Your plants are doing great." Zoe glanced at the potted plant on the table next to her. Its leaves were drooping. She made a mental note to water it.

"I didn't call to check up on the apartment. How are *you* doing?"

"I've been better," Zoe said. "I just got back from seeing my physical therapist."

Zoe recounted what Theo had told her, trying to hold back the sadness building inside her. Of course, that wasn't the only thing she was upset about. However, despite her closeness to Dawn, Zoe had never told her about Natasha. It would take too long to explain it all now. Hell, Zoe didn't even understand what was going on between them.

"I'm so sorry, Zoe," Dawn said. "I know how much ballet means to you. How are you holding up?"

"Not great," Zoe admitted. "I just feel so lost. Ballet has been my life for so long. I don't know what to do without it." She didn't even know what to do in the short term, let alone the rest of her life. She had no reason to go back to London any time soon. But did she have a reason to stay here?

"You don't have to do anything just yet. Take some time to rest and find your bearings again. You don't have to have all the answers right away."

"I guess."

"And, I know it feels like it right now, but this isn't the end of the world," Dawn said. "Just try to remember that, okay?"

Zoe sighed. "I'll try."

"You'll get through this. I'm sorry I can't be there for you. But I'll be thinking about you."

"Don't worry, I'll be fine."

In the background, someone yelled Dawn's name. "Crap. I have to go. But I'll talk to you as soon as I can. Probably in a few weeks. I love you."

"I love you too."

Zoe hung up and pulled out her earbuds. Talking to her big sister had made her feel a little better. But that knot of sadness deep in her stomach was still there.

A few minutes later, there was a knock on the door. The takeout Zoe ordered was here. Now that her career was over, she'd given up on eating healthy. She didn't have to follow her strict athlete diet any longer.

Zoe dragged herself up from the couch and opened her front door.

"Natasha?"

She stood before Zoe, her hair tied back, dressed in a familiar outfit of black tights and a long, black t-shirt underneath her open coat. Natasha always wore the same thing when teaching. Zoe had always wondered how she made something so plain look so elegant.

"I hope you don't mind me stopping by," Natasha said. "I wanted to talk to you in person."

"Sure," Zoe said. "Come in."

The two of them took a seat on the couch. Natasha had a

look of resolve plastered on her face. Could it be that she was nervous? Natasha had always been the type to hide her feelings behind a stone facade, but Zoe knew her well enough to be able to see through it. At least, Zoe had known her well. Was she still the same old Natasha?

"So," Zoe said. "What do you want to talk about?"

"I want to apologize for the other night," Natasha said. "I'm sorry for running out on you like that. The truth is, I was having such a great time just being here with you. I was surprised by how strong that connection between us still was. And all of a sudden, it was like the past came flooding back."

Zoe had felt it too, that night. The moment Natasha had touched her, it was like she was reliving all those little moments when their unspoken attraction had almost boiled over.

"But back then, I wasn't supposed to have any feelings for you," Natasha said. "I tried so hard to repress them that even now, my instinct was to pull away from you. And the last time we saw each other, when you came to my house, I handled everything so badly. I never meant to hurt you."

"It's okay," Zoe said. "There are no hard feelings there." She meant it. And the last thing she wanted to talk about was that night. At least, not yet. "It's all in the past. Let's just forget about it."

"For what it's worth, I'm sorry."

"It's no big deal. Let's just start fresh."

Natasha's relief was palpable. "At least let me make it up to you for the other night."

"What do you mean?" Zoe asked.

"I want to take you out on a date."

A date with Natasha? And a real one, not just some last-minute dinner. It was the kind of thing Zoe had only ever dreamed about, in between her other fantasies of Natasha which were of a much naughtier kind.

"Well?" Natasha said. "Will you go on a date with me?"

"Yes," Zoe stammered. "Of course."

"How about tomorrow night?"

"That's perfect."

"Great, I'll pick you up at seven." Natasha glanced at her phone. "I can't stay. I have a class soon. I need to get back to work."

Zoe walked Natasha to the door, her heart racing. A date with Natasha. It was almost enough to make her forget all about the events of the day.

"I'll see you tomorrow," Natasha said. "I'm looking forward to it."

Zoe smiled. "I can't wait."

The two of them lingered in the doorway as if held there by some force. Moments passed in silence. Then, Natasha reached out, took Zoe's chin in her fingers, and kissed her.

Zoe closed her eyes. It was a fleeting, gentle touch of the lips, just a shadow of a real kiss, but it was enough to send heat coursing through Zoe's veins. When Natasha broke away, Zoe's lips tried to follow.

Natasha brushed one of Zoe's curls back. "Tomorrow," she said softly.

The look in Natasha's eyes told Zoe all she needed to know.

6

NATASHA

*A*fter a month or so of lessons together, the tension between Natasha and Zoe had slowly eased. The secrets they'd shared had changed something between them. Natasha had started to see Zoe as more than just another student. She was a young woman with dreams and desires, doubts and fears. And Zoe seemed to be warming up to Natasha. Did she see Natasha differently too?

However, they were making frustratingly little progress when it came to Zoe's dancing. She was still as inconsistent as ever. During their last lesson, Natasha had felt like they were finally starting to get somewhere. Today, it was like all her progress had been undone.

Natasha didn't understand it. Zoe was so flighty and changeable, and Natasha couldn't figure out why. For someone like Natasha who thrived on order, it was infuriating.

"Stop." Natasha clapped her hands. "I can see the effort behind every step you make. I can see the gears turning in your head. Where is that effortless lightness that I know you're capable of? What's going on?"

"I don't know!" Zoe said. "I can't help it. You keep telling me to focus on this or that. I'm trying, but I just can't get anything right."

"Am I giving you too many corrections at once?"

"No, that's not it. It's just that, I know I should be able to do this. I've done it before a million times. But I keep screwing up, and then I get frustrated, and that just makes me screw up even more."

Natasha pursed her lips in thought. "You dance better when you're in a good mood, don't you?"

"Well, yeah," Zoe said. "Doesn't everyone?"

"Not the same way you do," Natasha said. "I think I get it now. You're a feeler, not a thinker. You dance with your heart and not your head. Me telling you to focus isn't going to get us anywhere. Instead, what we should be doing is harnessing all that passion and emotion you feel to lift you up so that you're in the right mindset."

"And how do we do that?"

Natasha thought for a moment. "What's your favorite ballet?"

The Sleeping Beauty," Zoe replied.

"Why? What do you like about it?"

"I loved fairy tales as a kid, and it was one of my favorites. I love how the ballet goes a lot deeper into the story. And, I guess I like the romance of it all. Plus, it's the first ballet I ever saw."

"Tell me some more about going to see it," Natasha said. "How old were you? Who did you go with?"

"I was six. My parents took my sister and me. I

remember thinking it would be boring, like that time they'd dragged us to go see a play." A faraway look crossed Zoe's face. "That night changed my whole life."

"Is that what got you interested in ballet?"

"Yes. I was hooked from the moment Aurora appeared on stage. As soon as the show was over, I told my parents I wanted to be a ballerina when I grew up. They enrolled me in classes the very next day."

"Do you remember what that was like?" Natasha asked. "To be six years old, watching the dancers on stage?"

"It was incredible," Zoe said. "It was like I was transported into this whole other world full of beauty and wonder. It was like magic."

Natasha placed her hand on Zoe's arm lightly. "Shut your eyes."

When Zoe's eyes were closed, Natasha went to the stereo and searched through the collection of CDs until she found what she was looking for. She slid it in and pressed play. The waltz from Sleeping Beauty rang out through the speakers.

Natasha turned the volume up, letting the music echo through the studio. When she returned to Zoe's side, her student had a soft smile on her face.

"Listen to the music," Natasha said. "How does it make you feel?

"Like—" Zoe chewed her lip. "Like I can soar."

"That's right. Just like dance, music has the power to provoke strong feelings. And music is connected to memory. Music speaks to the soul. We can harness that when you dance. Let the music guide you. Let it center you. Focus on the music, and everything else will fall into place."

Zoe stood there, eyes closed, breathing softly. Natasha had never seen her so still and serene. It was a stark contrast to the flighty, jumpy Zoe from moments ago.

The song ended. "How do you feel now?" Natasha asked.

"I feel good. Lighter, somehow." Zoe opened her eyes and stared at Natasha. "This might actually work."

"You sound so surprised."

"I guess I wasn't expecting you to come up with such a creative solution."

"I wouldn't be a very good teacher if I wasn't flexible," Natasha said. "My job is to help my students reach their full potential, not to try to fit them into a box. And you have so much potential."

Zoe looked at Natasha curiously, apparently surprised by the compliment. Natasha had always been sparing with her praise of Zoe. She'd didn't want her student to become complacent. Zoe had real talent. If she pushed herself, she could achieve great things. And Natasha was determined to see her succeed.

Lately, Natasha had become more and more invested in Zoe's success. But it was only natural. Zoe was her first private student.

That was all it was.

Natasha walked back over to the stereo. "Here. Give this a try." She selected another track from *The Sleeping Beauty*, a fast-paced piece from the climax, and rattled off a long, complex list of steps for Zoe to perform.

"Seriously?" Zoe said.

"You can do it." It was challenging, especially at the tempo of the music that was playing. But Zoe could do it. "Give it a try."

Natasha counted Zoe in. Zoe performed the exercise shakily, her face screwed up in concentration.

"Good," Natasha said. "You have the basic steps down. Now try it again. But this time, don't think about what you're doing. Feel the music. Feel what you're doing in relation to it and adjust. I'll go easy on the corrections for now."

Natasha counted Zoe in again. Zoe performed the steps again, this time with a lot more confidence.

"Yes, to arabesque," Natasha said. "Again." She didn't want to give Zoe a chance to rest. She didn't want her to lose momentum.

With every repetition, Zoe got better and better. Every leap was lighter, every pirouette perfectly balanced. Natasha had never pushed Zoe that hard before. But Zoe rose to the challenge.

"Much better!" Natasha said. "This time, keep your shoulders back. Again."

Natasha watched her carefully, dissecting her every movement. There was very little for her to correct. Zoe had never danced so perfectly before. Had they finally made a breakthrough?

"Stop," Natasha finally said.

Zoe put her hand on her knees, breathing hard. "How was that?"

Natasha stared at her. Watching Zoe dance just now had filled her with this exhilarating warmth that was like nothing she'd ever felt. Even seeing Paige dance, years ago when she'd been in her prime, was nothing compared to this.

"That was good," Natasha said. "But we can do better."

Zoe nodded and straightened up. "Let's keep going."

It seemed Zoe wasn't at risk of losing her drive any time soon. But Natasha didn't want to push her too hard. "That's enough for tonight. But we still have a few minutes." She folded her arms across her chest. "You have an audition in San Francisco coming up. Let's talk about that."

7

NATASHA

Natasha parked her car in front of Zoe's apartment. She was early. Knowing Zoe, she wouldn't be ready yet. Natasha pulled her phone out of her purse. It had buzzed while she was driving. She had two emails. One was from work.

The other was from her mom.

How had her mother even gotten her email address? She hadn't spoken to either of her parents since she was eighteen. That wasn't quite true. For the first year after Natasha had left home, both she and her parents had made attempts to reconcile. But her parents had refused to back down, and their conversations always devolved into fights, which only fractured their relationship even more. After a while, Natasha had stopped trying. She hadn't heard from them in almost twenty years.

Natasha opened the email. It was formal and straight to the point. That was typical of her mother. The email stated that she and Natasha's father were going to be in the city in a couple of weeks.

And they wanted to see her.

Her parents lived hundreds of miles away. Why were they coming here? And why would they want to see her after so long?

Did Natasha want to see them? She could say no. Or she could ignore them. But what if her parents really did want to mend their relationship this time? What if they'd finally gotten over Natasha's 'betrayal,' as they had put it? What if they'd finally decided to accept her for who she was and the choices she'd made? Despite everything, a part of her still wanted their approval. And a part of her wondered if she'd made the right decision by turning her back on them.

And Natasha hated herself for being so weak.

She sighed. She would deal with it later. Natasha got out of her car, made her way up to Zoe's apartment, and knocked on the door.

"Coming," Zoe yelled from somewhere inside. Moments later, the door swung open. "Natasha, come in. I'm just trying to find my heels."

Natasha followed Zoe inside. She couldn't help but stare at the other woman as she fluttered into the living room in search of her heels. Zoe was wearing a pale blue dress made of layers of chiffon. It was cut low at both the back and front, but her small chest made it seem modest. The lightweight dress emphasized the graceful way Zoe moved, as though she was floating instead of walking. All ballet dancers moved like that on stage. But with Zoe, it was like she was always in the middle of a show, dancing the part of a sylph, or a forest spirit, or some other ethereal creature that was so common in classical ballets.

After all this time, Zoe was still able to cast a spell on Natasha.

"There." Zoe made a beeline across the room in a flurry of fabric and pulled her high heels out from underneath the side table. She sat down and slipped them on. "So, where are we going?"

"We're going to the symphony," Natasha said. "Do you still like classical music?"

Zoe's face lit up. "Yes, of course."

"I have season tickets." It was one of Natasha's few indulgences. "Usually I take along a friend or someone from work. I thought you'd appreciate it more."

"That sounds perfect. I haven't had time to go in a long time. My job kept me too busy."

"We're going to dinner first, so I hope you're hungry."

"That sounds perfect," Zoe said. Without warning, she stood up and flung her arms around Natasha, planting a kiss on her cheek. "Let's go."

Natasha and Zoe took their seats in the concert hall. They had a little balcony at the back all to themselves.

Zoe gazed down at the stage where the orchestra was setting up, her eyes filled with childlike wonder. "I've been here a million times, but I've never sat up here before."

"It's far from the stage," Natasha said. "But the design of the hall means the acoustics are better here than anywhere else. These are the best seats in the house when it comes to sound."

Zoe looked at her and smiled. "This is nice. I'm having a really good time."

"Me too," Natasha said.

"And I love the restaurant we went to for dinner. It wasn't there when I lived here." A pensive look crossed Zoe's face. "The city has changed so much, but it still feels familiar. Comforting, almost."

"I know what you mean." Natasha didn't say so, but she felt that way about Zoe. Zoe had changed so much in the past ten years, yet being around her felt comfortable.

The lights dimmed, and the audience grew silent. Natasha settled back in her chair. The concert was about to start. Natasha glanced at Zoe. She looked happier than Natasha had seen her since they ran into each other at the grocery store. She simply glowed in a way that was so enthralling.

That was part of why Natasha was drawn to Zoe. Sure, she was beautiful. But it wasn't her looks Natasha was attracted to. It was her vibrant personality, and the way she could set the whole room alight when she danced, or even just smiled, like she was doing right now. As the orchestra began to play, Zoe closed her eyes, letting the music take her away. Natasha did the same.

The concert flew by in a whirlwind of sound and motion. Natasha felt a lot more at ease tonight than the other night at Zoe's apartment for dinner. She'd finally gotten over the surprise of seeing Zoe again, along with the realization that she still had feelings for her former student. And she felt a lot more in control now. That was one thing about Zoe that hadn't changed. She was this unpredictable force that turned Natasha's carefully ordered world upside down. That night at Zoe's apartment had done just that.

But maybe a little disruption to her life wasn't a bad thing.

When the last song on the program began, Natasha slipped her hand over to rest on Zoe's. Zoe looked at Natasha and smiled, then turned her attention back to the stage.

The piece ended. The crowd broke into rapturous applause. Naturally, Zoe leaped to her feet as she clapped. After an endless stream of bows, the symphony sat back down for an encore. The first notes rang out, the beginning of an unknown song. The somber, haunting melody was familiar, but Natasha couldn't place it at first. It was a song from a ballet, but she couldn't remember which one.

Did Zoe recognize it? Natasha turned to look at her. Only then did she notice that Zoe's whole body had grown stiff. Her face was barely visible in the dim light, but Natasha could see the pain written on it. And as the music rose, Natasha remembered what ballet the song was from. *Giselle*. That was the last ballet Zoe had danced in.

Natasha cursed herself. If she'd known the orchestra was going to play a piece from *Giselle*, she wouldn't have brought Zoe along. But even for someone as sensitive as Zoe, her reaction seemed disproportionate. Was something else going on?

Natasha squeezed Zoe's hand. Zoe drew it back into her lap. Natasha tried to get her attention. But all Zoe did was sit there, staring down at her feet.

Finally, the song ended. The audience got up and applauded once more. Zoe didn't join them this time. When the lights came on and everyone started to file out, Zoe stayed in her seat.

"Zoe?" Natasha ventured. "Are you alright?"

"Yeah." Zoe's eyes were glossy with tears. "I just wasn't expecting to hear that song."

"I'm sorry. I didn't know they were going to play it."

"No, it's fine. It's not just the song." Zoe sniffed. "I went to see my physical therapist yesterday. He told me I'm going to be out of action for the next three months. After that, it'll be too late for me to go back."

"Oh Zoe," Natasha said. "I'm sorry."

"I'm never going to dance on stage again."

"You don't know that."

"Don't try to make this all better," Zoe said. "My career is over. It's all over."

Natasha reached out and wiped a tear from Zoe's cheek. "Zoe, your career isn't over. There are other options. And you'll still be able to dance. Even if you're not a principal anymore, or even with the same company, you'll find a way."

"You sound so certain," Zoe said.

"I am certain. The Zoe I know wouldn't give up on her passion, no matter what."

Zoe sighed. "You're right. I'm sorry. I didn't mean to ruin our date."

"You haven't ruined anything." Natasha looked down at the hall. It was empty now. They'd been sitting here for a while. "Come on. Let's get out of here."

"Okay."

As Natasha reached down for her purse on the floor beneath her, she felt Zoe's hand on hers.

"Natasha?" Zoe said quietly.

Natasha straightened up. Before she knew what was happening, Zoe leaned over and brought her lips to Natasha's in a gentle, inquiring kiss. A ripple of desire went through Natasha's body. Zoe's lips were so soft, and the skin of her neck and cheek was like velvet under Natasha's fingertips. Somewhere inside, she began to pulse and flare with need.

Natasha broke away. "Let me take you home."

8
ZOE

Natasha handed Zoe a glass of water and sat down on the couch next to her. It was late now, but the moon was out in full, bathing the living room in gentle light through the wide window.

"Feeling better?" Natasha asked.

"Yeah," Zoe said. "You seem to have that effect on me."

Natasha gave her a subdued smile. She was so entrancing. She wore a long dress with thin straps in a shade of navy blue that looked striking against her pale skin. The outfit was accented by a delicate silver pendant with matching earrings. She'd always dressed in this simple way that only heightened her natural elegance.

Zoe's heart thumped like mad. The kiss they'd shared had left her with a yearning stronger than anything she'd ever felt before. She'd wanted Natasha for so long. Even back when Zoe's attraction to her had been nothing more than tinder waiting for a spark, she'd felt this pull toward Natasha that she didn't understand. And once Zoe had realized what it was, she'd also realized that it could never be more than a dream.

At least, not until now.

"Are you sure you're all right?" Natasha asked.

"Yes," Zoe said. "I just got lost in my head for a second."

"What were you thinking about?"

Zoe's words came out as a breathy whisper. "I was thinking about how much I want you."

Natasha was still and silent. For a moment, Zoe wondered if she had been too forward once again. But when she looked into Natasha's eyes, she saw desire swirling within them, dark as a storm.

Then, Natasha leaned in and covered Zoe's lips with her own.

Zoe closed her eyes and melted into the kiss. Natasha's hand swept up the side of Zoe's neck, the other sliding up her thigh. She quivered. When they'd kissed on this couch the other night, Zoe had been left wondering if Natasha wanted her at all. Now there was no doubt about it. Zoe could feel Natasha's passion in every brush of her fingers and press of her lips.

Zoe ran her hands down Natasha's sides, feeling her curves through the thin fabric of her dress. More than once, she had imagined what Natasha's curves would feel like. But she'd never dreamed they'd be so soft and supple.

Natasha pushed Zoe back against the arm of the couch. The weight of the other woman's body against Zoe's made her weak. Natasha's hands roamed over the outlines of Zoe's body with the lightest of touches. It wasn't tentative or hesitant. It was measured and tender, as if Natasha wanted to take her time.

But Zoe didn't want to take her time. She'd waited ten years for this. She skirted her palm up Natasha's waist to caress the side of her breast. Her other hand slid down to the swell of Natasha's ass cheek.

"Natasha," Zoe said, every syllable laced with desperation. "I want you."

Natasha's breath hitched. She reached down to strip Zoe's dress from her shoulders, then dragged the front of it down, exposing Zoe's bare breasts to the cool air. She rarely wore bras. She didn't have much to support. And judging by Natasha's hungry gaze, she didn't mind Zoe's bralessness.

Natasha drew her fingertips across Zoe's breasts, causing her nipples to stiffen. Natasha dipped down to kiss her again, then grazed her lips along the side of Zoe's neck, over her collarbone and down her breast until she reached its tip. She swirled her tongue around it, sucking it firmly. Zoe arched her chest up toward her.

When she couldn't take any more, Zoe groped for the hem of Natasha's dress and pulled it up, wanting to bury herself in the other woman's warm, milky skin. Natasha did the rest, straightening up and tugging her dress up off her head. Underneath, she wore a set of matching deep-red underwear, in a style as simple as her dress and just as alluring.

Zoe gaped at her shamelessly. Did Natasha know how many times Zoe had fantasized about this moment? How many nights she'd lain awake, wondering what it would be like to feel Natasha's body against hers?

She pulled Natasha back down to her, their lips and bodies crushing together. She reached around to unclip Natasha's bra and stripped it from her shoulders, tossing it aside to join the rest of their clothes strewn across the floor. She skimmed her hands up to Natasha's breasts, a nipple sliding between the insides of her fingers.

A murmur rose from Natasha's chest. She shifted atop Zoe, positioning herself between Zoe's legs. The press of Natasha's hips, grinding against her, made Zoe throb.

"Natasha," she said. "I want you."

Once again, Zoe's words galvanized Natasha. She trailed her hand up the inside of Zoe's legs and up to her panties, stroking the heat where Zoe's thighs met. Zoe whimpered, straining into her. Natasha's torturous slowness had gone from sweet to agonizing.

Natasha drew her hand back up and slipped them into the top of Zoe's panties, then ran her fingers down to brush Zoe's slit. "How much?" she asked. "How much do you want me?"

Zoe let out a sharp breath. "I don't just want you, Natasha. I *need* you."

Zoe could feel the shift that went through Natasha's body at her words. Natasha grabbed the waistband of Zoe's panties and yanked them from her legs. A second later, Natasha was on her again, pushing her knees even further apart. Zoe lay one foot on the floor, the other bent against the back of the couch.

Natasha slid her fingers down between Zoe's lips again, circling her entrance. Zoe trembled. Slowly, Natasha entered her, piercing her to her core. Zoe gasped and reached up blindly, grabbing hold of Natasha's waist to anchor herself.

Still buried inside Zoe, Natasha shifted down to caress

her breasts with her lips and tongue. Zoe relaxed and let pleasure overtake her. This was so much better than she'd imagined. And she'd imagined it so many times. Late at night, in bed alone in the dark, her own hands working frantically, she'd imagined Natasha's body against hers, just like now. She'd imagined Natasha's hand between her thighs, and her mouth on her breasts and on her lips and neck, just like right now. And she'd writhed on the bed, lost in ecstasy, just like right now. And she would whisper Natasha's name into the dark as she came closer and closer to release.

"Natasha," Zoe said softly.

Natasha picked up the pace, her fingers surging inside, the heel of her palm nudging at Zoe's clit. Moments later, Zoe let out a piercing cry, her head tipping back over the arm of the couch as she shattered against Natasha's body. Natasha held her close, still inside her, until her orgasm subsided.

Zoe drew Natasha in and kissed her. Still lost in a haze of bliss, Natasha's lips felt heavenly. Her hands wandered down Natasha's body once more, one hand gliding down to the peak of her thighs. The dark panties she still wore were wet. Zoe guided her fingers inside them and into Natasha's slit. Natasha shuddered atop her.

"You want to know how much I want you?" Zoe said. "Let me show you."

Natasha took in a breath, her chest rising. Zoe slipped off the couch and sank to her knees before the other woman. She was still weak from her orgasm, but she hungered for a taste of Natasha. She ran her hands up the sides of Natasha's legs until she reached the waist of

Natasha's panties. Natasha lifted her hips so that Zoe could pull them off.

Wordlessly, Natasha slid to the edge of the couch. Zoe nudged Natasha's legs apart and gazed up at her face. Her cheeks were flushed crimson and her lips were parted slightly.

Zoe spread Natasha's lower lips out, feeling their silky heat with her fingers, and traced Natasha's folds. She snaked her fingertips over the other woman's hard, pink nub. Natasha moaned.

Zoe leaned in. The woman's scent was so divine. She pressed her tongue to Natasha's folds, licking upward in long, lazy strokes, savoring the taste of her arousal. Natasha shifted forward again, pushing into Zoe's mouth, her hands falling to the back of Zoe's head.

Zoe painted her tongue up Natasha's slit, feeling for her hidden bud. As soon as she uncovered it, she swirled her tongue around it, softly at first, then a little harder.

Natasha rolled back against her, her hand lacing through Zoe's hair. "God, yes."

Zoe grabbed onto the insides of Natasha's thighs, working her mouth harder between them. She attuned to Natasha's body's responses, learning what made her gasp and moan. Soon, Zoe had Natasha shaking on the couch.

"Oh god, Zoe. Oh, god!" Natasha arched out, her thighs hugging Zoe's head, her whole body quaking.

Zoe kept going until Natasha's body grew calm.

Zoe snuggled up to Natasha on the couch. "You're quiet."

"It's just been a while since I've done that," Natasha said. "I mean, had a chance to really let go."

Zoe ran a hand up Natasha's stomach to her chest. There was a hint of tension in her body. "Are you sure that's all?"

Natasha kissed the top of Zoe's head. "Maybe there's still a part of me that finds it hard to stop thinking about you as someone who was off limits."

"It's hard for me to stop thinking about you that way too." Zoe grinned. "But there's nothing wrong with that."

Natasha shook her head. Nevertheless, Zoe could feel the tightness release from Natasha's body.

"You know, I fantasized about this so many times," Zoe said.

"Really? And what did you fantasize about?"

"It's... personal."

"Oh, now I'm curious. You have to tell me."

Zoe hesitated. "Most of my fantasies took place in the studio where we had our lessons."

"*Fantasies?*" Natasha said. "As in more than one?"

"You wanted me to tell you, didn't you?" Zoe crossed her arms.

"Okay, go on."

"They started off as lessons like any other. But then things got..." Zoe glanced down into her lap. "Let's just say, one of them involved you tying me to the barre."

There was a flash of amusement in Natasha's dark eyes. "You're serious?"

"You said you wanted to know." Zoe pouted. "This is why I didn't want to tell you."

"I'm not judging you." Natasha drew Zoe in closer. "I just had no idea you thought about me that way."

"What, you mean sexually? Didn't you ever think about me that way?"

"No, never. I couldn't allow myself to. That was a path I could never go down."

"Right." Zoe wasn't surprised. Back then, Natasha had never acknowledged her feelings for Zoe. Neither of them had, not until it was too late. But still, Zoe couldn't help but feel hurt. Had Natasha never taken her feelings seriously?

"Zoe, it was different for you," Natasha said. "You weren't the one in a position of power. I would never want to abuse that."

"I'm pretty sure I made it very clear that you wouldn't have been taking advantage," Zoe said. "It's not like we weren't both adults."

"You were barely an adult."

"Right. I was just some stupid teenager to you."

"No," Natasha said. "You were my student. If I ever seemed dismissive of you, it was because I was trying to maintain some level of professionalism. Our relationship was inappropriate. We were both lonely, and lost, and turned to each other for comfort when we shouldn't have."

Zoe pulled away, disentangling herself from Natasha's arms. "You think we were just using each other?"

"I didn't mean—" Natasha pinched her lips together. "What I mean is, it wasn't right that I put you in a position where I was confiding in you about my personal life. You can't tell me that was healthy. I should have never let things go that far."

"Maybe it was unhealthy," Zoe said. "But I never thought we were just using each other. I never thought that everything we had was just because we were lonely. All those times I bared my soul to you. Do you really just see it as some kind of lapse in judgment? Do you think everything between us was a mistake?"

"No, of course not."

"Maybe you're right. Maybe we were using each other. Maybe I did the exact same thing tonight, dragging you back home with me and having sex with you to make myself feel better about all the other crap that's going on in my life."

"Zoe—"

"You should leave."

Natasha didn't protest. She simply got up and gathered her clothes. Zoe watched her in silence.

Once Natasha was dressed, she turned back to Zoe. "All I'm trying to say is that I was your teacher, and I should have never crossed that line with a student. But that doesn't mean what we had didn't mean anything to me."

Zoe scowled. "Just go."

"Fine." Without another word, Natasha picked up her purse and left Zoe's apartment.

9
ZOE

For Zoe, there hadn't been one moment when she'd crossed that line with Natasha. It had been a slow, gradual thing. But she could pinpoint the moment she'd realized it. And by then, it had been too late.

It was the Monday after Zoe's audition for the San Francisco Ballet. She'd dragged herself to her lesson with Natasha, feeling completely dejected. The audition had been a complete disaster.

She hadn't been looking forward to facing Natasha. She felt like she'd let her down. Zoe didn't think that Natasha would be disappointed in her. But they had worked so hard together. They'd spent weeks getting ready, staying late after every lesson, refining Zoe's technique and preparing her for everything the audition could possibly throw at her.

It hadn't been enough.

Zoe entered the studio. Natasha was sitting on the bench to the side, looking through paperwork.

She looked up at her student. "Zoe. How did the audition go?"

Zoe just shook her head.

"What happened?" Natasha asked.

"I don't know." Zoe collapsed on the bench next to her. "I started out okay, but then I made a mistake, and it threw me off completely. Then it was all downhill from there."

"It's only natural that you'd make a few mistakes at an audition. The judges don't expect perfection."

"It was more than a few mistakes. It was just... everything was so off." Zoe held her head in her hands. "I don't know what happened. I've been doing so well in the past few weeks. The exercises the judges threw at us, they should have been easy. It was nothing I wasn't prepared for. But I just couldn't dance like I could in lessons. And I don't understand why."

"I'm sorry, Zoe. I know you had high hopes for this audition."

"It wasn't just this audition. It's every other audition I've been to." Zoe threw her hands up. "It's so frustrating. I can do this. I know I can. I've spent my entire life working toward this. I've been dancing since I was six. I've been going to classes daily since I was eight. I've sacrificed so much. I don't have friends, or a social life, or hobbies. I've never had a girlfriend or been to prom. I missed out on all that normal teenage stuff, just so I could pursue my dream. And I don't regret any of it. Ballet is my life. There's nothing else I'd rather be doing." Her voice cracked. "But what if, in the end, it was all for nothing?"

"Zoe," Natasha said. "It won't be for nothing. This was one audition. Even if you don't get in this time, there will be other opportunities."

"That's the thing. I'm almost nineteen. I need to join a

company soon if I'm ever going to have a chance at making it big. But there aren't many more auditions left this year. I'm running out of chances."

"There are still other options. Like competitions. The World Grand Prix is coming up. Do well there, and you won't need to audition. You'll have scouts knocking on your door with offers."

Zoe groaned. "I can't even perform well at auditions. How am I supposed to perform at a competition in front of all those people without screwing up?"

"We can work on that."

"How?"

"Let me worry about that," Natasha said. "It's my job, after all."

"Okay." Zoe sighed. "I don't know if there's any point having a lesson right now. I'm too much of a mess to dance. Sorry, I should have canceled."

"It's okay. Maybe an evening off will do you some good."

Natasha placed a reassuring hand on Zoe's arm. A jolt of electricity shot through her. Zoe didn't know why Natasha's touch made her feel that way. Natasha was always touching her, on her shoulders, her stomach, her hips, and her legs. It the simplest way for a teacher to correct a student's form. There was nothing unusual about it. But lately, when Natasha touched her, it made her skin sizzle.

Natasha must have felt it too. She pulled her hand away. They sat there in silence. Since their lesson was canceled, Zoe didn't have a reason not to get up and go home. But she found herself wanting to stay.

Natasha finally spoke. "Since you're here anyway, why don't we do something else? Something fun."

"Like what?" 'Fun' wasn't a word she associated with Natasha.

"Like—" Natasha thought for a moment. "Let's go get ice cream."

"Ice cream? Are you forgetting I'm not one of the ten-year-olds you teach?"

"It might make you feel better. When I used to dance, my teacher would take us out for ice cream to reward us after performances and competitions. Even if we did badly, she said that just getting through it was an achievement. And I always liked it, even as I got older." Natasha folded her arms across her chest. "So, are you coming?"

Zoe looked around the ice cream parlor. It was evening, but the cold weather meant the cozy little shop was almost empty. The only other customers were a young man and a woman sitting nearby, laughing and smiling together. They looked like they were on a date.

Natasha eyed Zoe's sundae, a mountain of ice cream in three different flavors topped with nuts and chocolate sauce. "Weren't you just saying that ice cream was for kids?"

Zoe shrugged. "You know how it is. I never get to eat this stuff. Might as well go a little crazy." She picked up her spoon. "Do you want some? They gave us two spoons after all."

"Probably because they didn't believe all that ice cream was for one person," Natasha said. "I'll stick to coffee."

"Suit yourself." Zoe took a bite of her sundae and murmured with bliss. "This is really good. If you want to keep taking me out for ice cream in place of our lessons, I won't complain."

"Then I'd have to take all my students out for ice cream. I wouldn't want to show favoritism."

"No one else has to know. We can start our own tradition. Just the two of us."

A shadow of a smile crossed Natasha's face. "I'll think about it."

"So," Zoe said. "Your old ballet teacher used to do this? Take you out for ice cream?"

"Yes. She was old-school. Very strict. This was her one concession to her usual no-nonsense attitude. I think she understood how stressful being a young ballet dancer is, and how much pressure we faced. She recognized that we needed some downtime every now and then."

"Old-school and strict, huh?" Zoe said. "That explains a lot."

Natasha raised an eyebrow. "What are you implying?"

"Nothing."

"Trust me, I'm nowhere near as strict as she was."

"Right." Zoe took another bite of her sundae and nudged the bowl across the table in Natasha's direction. "Are you sure you don't want some?"

Natasha hesitated, then picked up the spoon. "Why not?"

"So," Zoe said. "You used to dance? Seriously, I mean?"

Natasha nodded. "Until I was seventeen."

That didn't surprise Zoe. Lots of ballet teachers were former dancers. Natasha's knowledge of ballet could only have come from studying it religiously for most of her life.

"Why did you stop?" Zoe asked.

"I got to that age where it was do or die," Natasha said. "I was faced with the choice to either pursue ballet seriously or bow out. As much as I loved ballet, I was cursed with the wrong body type."

Zoe knew what Natasha meant. The ideal ballet dancer was slim and long-limbed, with no hips or chest to speak of. It was one of the harsh realities of ballet. It hadn't escaped Zoe's notice that Natasha was curvier than the average ballet dancer. That wasn't a bad thing in her opinion. More than once, while she did her warm-up stretches, Zoe had caught herself staring at Natasha in the mirror. Lately, Natasha's presence alone seemed to stir something deep within her.

"I realized I was never going to make it, so I stopped," Natasha continued. "I decided to focus on school instead so I could get into a good college. At least, that was the plan. But sometimes, life takes you in unexpected directions. I ended up teaching ballet instead."

"Was it hard?" Zoe asked. "Giving up on ballet?"

"Yes, of course. I'd worked hard at it my whole life. I loved it."

"How did you know it was the right decision?"

"It just felt right." Natasha narrowed her eyes. "You're not thinking about giving up, are you?"

"No. I mean, after the audition, I considered it. But I don't think I could ever give up ballet."

"Good. Because you're far more talented than I ever was."

Zoe smiled. "Thanks again for this. You're right. I needed a break. And it's nice to have someone to talk to who understands this stuff. Most people don't understand that ballet is a 24/7 job."

"I haven't forgotten what that's like," Natasha said. "It can be isolating."

"Yeah." Zoe felt more alone than ever right now. At least in the past, she'd had her sister to talk to about everything, but Dawn was still away.

"How are things going with the other students at the academy? Have all those rumors died down?"

"Mostly. I still get dirty looks in the changing rooms sometimes. But I'm used to being an outsider, so dealing with that kind of thing is nothing new."

"You said that once before," Natasha said. "That you're used to being an outsider."

"Well, yeah. When it comes to the ballet world, I don't fit in for obvious reasons."

"What do you mean?"

Zoe raised an eyebrow. "How many Black ballet dancers do you see? Especially at the elite level?"

"Not many. Huh. I guess I never noticed."

"Well, it's a lot more noticeable to me. Ballet has always had this obsession with its dancers looking the same. You know, that pale, slim, white swan look. Anyone who doesn't fit into that box has a hard time getting anywhere. And there are people who are a lot less subtle about their views when it comes to anyone who's 'different.'"

"Even at the academy?" Natasha asked.

"Especially at the academy. I've been putting up with all kinds of crap since I was little. Although it was mostly the moms rather than the other kids. Like, whenever I wore my natural hair to class, they'd make snide comments about how 'messy' it was. They seriously expected twelve-year-old me to straighten my hair all the time just so I'd look the way they thought a dancer should look? And then there was that time one of the moms tried to get me kicked out of my role as one of the snowflakes in *The Nutcracker* because I 'ruined the aesthetic.' Although, she might have just been mad her kid only got a background role."

"Christ, I had no idea that kind of thing was going on."

"It's not a big deal," Zoe said. "I mean, it doesn't bother me most of the time. I've grown a thick skin over the years."

"Why don't you ever say something? You could go to the director."

"When I was younger, my mom used to make a big deal out of anything she caught wind of. You should have seen her after the snowflake incident. She dragged me into the director's office and made him apologize and promise he wouldn't let anything like that ever happen at the school again. All that did was make everyone say those things behind my back rather than right in front of me," Zoe muttered.

"I can't imagine how hard that must be," Natasha said.

Zoe shrugged. "I can handle it. I mean, it sucks, but it doesn't help to sit here crying about it." Her hands tightened into fists. "I'm going to prove all those people wrong. I'm going to earn my place at the top and show everyone who tried to stop me that I belong there. They're all going to eat their words when I'm dancing for the New York Ballet."

"Good for you," Natasha said. "With your talent and passion, it won't be long before you get there."

"Thanks." Zoe bit the inside of her lip. Natasha rarely praised her when it came to her dancing. "It means a lot, you know. That you believe in me."

"Of course I do," Natasha said. "Do you really think I'd

be staying late in the studio with you every lesson if I didn't think you have what it takes to make it? You have a bright future ahead of you. But you're going to have to work for it."

"Of course. I will."

Natasha nodded toward the sundae between them. "We should finish this before it melts."

"Right." Zoe picked up her spoon. She had that fluttery feeling in her stomach again. Was this some kind of crush? On Natasha? Not only was she Zoe's teacher, but it seemed like yesterday that the two of them had been butting heads every time they had a lesson.

Whatever this was, Zoe would have to be careful not to let it get out of hand.

10

NATASHA

*N*atasha remembered the exact moment she'd crossed that line with Zoe. It was the first time she'd realized Zoe meant more to her than just a student.

After that evening in the ice cream parlor, Zoe had made great strides in her classes with Natasha. They were due to have another lesson in just a few minutes. But that evening, Natasha was the one who was unprepared.

She sat in her car in the parking lot by the academy. She'd spent the afternoon attending a professional workshop, then she'd driven back to work, intent on getting some paperwork done before her lesson with Zoe. Instead, she'd spent the last ten minutes sitting in the front seat of her car, staring at nothing at all. There was only one person in the world who could rattle her like this.

Paige. Her ex-girlfriend.

Paige had been at that very same workshop. The dance community was small, so it was inevitable that Natasha would run into her eventually. Somehow, Natasha had managed to avoid her until now.

She sighed. She had to get it together, if not for her own sake, then for Zoe's. She had a lesson to teach. The last thing she needed was to fall apart now. She and Zoe were finally starting to make real progress.

Natasha looked at the time. Their lesson was due to start in five minutes. She got out of the car and headed inside. When she entered the studio, Zoe was already there, stretching at the barre.

Zoe smiled at her as she walked in. "Natasha. I've been working my fouettes like we talked about. I think I'm getting somewhere."

"Good." Natasha tried to mask the disquiet in her voice. "You can show me later."

Natasha placed her bag down and removed her coat, her back to Zoe. She was trying her hardest to keep herself together, but her mind was still going over her encounter with Paige. Paige had made it clear that she wanted Natasha back. She'd said she *needed* Natasha. That wasn't what unsettled her. As far as she was concerned, the two of them were done. What unsettled her was the sharp edge in Paige's voice, the insistent look in her eye.

"Natasha?" Zoe's voice cut through the still air.

"Yes?" Natasha spun around. Zoe was standing right behind her, and she hadn't even noticed.

"I said, I'm ready." Zoe put her hands on her hips. "What's the matter?"

"Nothing." Natasha did her best to hide the shaking in her voice. "Let's get started. Back to the barre."

Zoe didn't move. "Natasha, what's going on?"

"It's nothing that concerns you."

"Well, do you want to talk about it anyway?"

Natasha hesitated. Her student was the last person she should be talking to about her problems. Especially not this particular problem. But she had no one else. Paige had gotten all their mutual friends in the breakup. Zoe was one of the only people Natasha had left who even knew about Paige.

"You can talk to me, you know," Zoe said, reading her mind. "It's not like you haven't listened to me talk about all my problems before."

"It's different. You're my student."

"So what? We're both adults. And I want to help, even if it just means listening." Zoe lowered her gaze slightly. "When I talk to you, you make me feel understood. And you make me feel like I'm a little less alone in the world. Can't I return the favor?"

Natasha sighed and sat down. Zoe joined her on the bench. "It's nothing, really. I ran into my ex today at a work event. She's a dancer, so we run in the same circles professionally."

"Oh. Are you okay?"

"Yes. It just threw me, that's all."

"Did things between you end badly?" Zoe asked.

The way things had ended between Natasha and Paige couldn't begin to be covered by the word 'badly.' "Something like that," Natasha said. "It was very drawn out. Our relationship had been over for a while, at least on my end. I fell out of love with her long before we broke up. But it was hard to actually end it. We'd been together for so long, and I'd given up so much for her, that I wanted it to work out. It was irrational, but I felt like I had to stick it out to prove to myself and everyone else that I hadn't wasted over a decade of my life."

"It's not irrational," Zoe said. "It's hard to give up on something you've invested so much in. Or someone."

"What made it even harder was that Paige didn't want to give up on us," Natasha said. "I thought she'd accepted my decision in the end, but when I saw her today, she said she wanted me back. But things are well and truly over between us." Natasha clasped her hands in her lap. "And that's enough about my problems. Let's get started with the lesson."

"Wait, your ex is a dancer?" Zoe said slowly. "And her name is Paige?"

Natasha cursed herself. She'd slipped up by mentioning Paige's name. "Yes."

"Is your ex-girlfriend Paige *Collins*?"

"Yes," Natasha said. "She's that Paige. One of the biggest ballet stars of our generation." She was a former principal dancer for the Metro Ballet, the city's premier ballet company, and one of the best in the world. Paige had once been Metro's crown jewel. Her face, topped with that trademark blonde hair of hers, had been on posters and billboards around the city. Every ballet dancer in the world knew who she was. "So now you see why we kept our relationship secret all that time." Ballet's openness toward gay dancers didn't apply to female dancers. At least, it hadn't back when Natasha and Paige had gotten together.

"Yeah," Zoe said. "Wow. That must have been a hard secret to keep. I promise I won't tell a soul. And if you ever need to talk about it, I'm here."

"You're sweet," Natasha said. "But I'm fine."

"You're allowed to not be fine."

Natasha stared at Zoe. She seemed to understand Natasha on a level she would never have expected. But like Zoe said, they were both adults. There was nothing wrong with the closeness growing between them.

At least, in theory.

"We should get back to the lesson." Natasha stood up. "But first, let's talk about the World Grand Prix."

The World Grand Prix was the most prestigious international ballet competition for aspiring ballet dancers. Only the best qualified for it, and Zoe had just scraped through this year. Winning the Grand Prix wasn't everything. The competition was attended by scouts from ballet companies all over the world. The real prize, at least for the older competitors, was to be recruited by a ballet company.

"Have you thought about what you want to perform?" Natasha asked.

"Something classic," Zoe said. "But I don't know what, exactly."

"We should play to your strengths. Choose something that grabs you, really moves you. That speaks to your heart." Natasha pursed her lips in thought. "Something from *The Sleeping Beauty*?"

"That's a great idea. How about one of Aurora's solos?"

Of course Zoe would choose one of the star's solos. "The wedding from the final act?" Natasha said. "It'll definitely impress."

"I've always liked the one from the second act better."

"Ah. When Aurora appears as a vision, conjured for her prince."

"That's the one," Zoe said. "It was always my favorite part."

"It's a beautiful piece. It suits you." Zoe was a dreamer. And when she danced, she was a beautiful vision, like some magic in motion. "All right. That's settled. Let's get started."

Zoe nodded and walked over to the barre, awaiting Natasha's instructions.

The words left Natasha's mouth before she had a chance to think. "I'm coming with you to the competition."

"You are?" Zoe said.

"Yes. As your coach."

A grin broke out on Zoe's face. "That's great. Thank you!"

"I'm just doing my job." It was all within the bounds of Natasha's job description. It wasn't unusual for a teacher to go along to competitions with a student, especially if they were being taught privately. And the Grand Prix just happened to be right here in the city, so it wasn't like Natasha would have to go out of her way.

Natasha going along to support Zoe as her coach. That was all it was.

11
NATASHA

Natasha said goodbye to the last of her students. Her final class for the day was over. She usually taught a private lesson after her group class, but her student had canceled.

It was rare that she had an evening off. She didn't know what to do with herself. At some point over the past few years, her job had become her whole life. Natasha liked her job, and she'd worked hard to get to where she was. But it was all she had.

It hadn't always been this way. It was like one day, she'd woken up and begun to notice how tedious it all was. She'd lived in the same city for twenty-odd years, and in the same house for most of that time. All her friends were also her colleagues. She was almost forty and still single. And she couldn't remember the last time she'd had a relationship that lasted more than a handful of months.

Natasha sat down at the bench at the side of the studio. She'd had a real shot at something with Zoe, and she'd messed it up. Natasha hadn't spoken to her since the other night when Zoe had kicked her out. Natasha didn't even know how to begin fixing everything. She hadn't meant to suggest she'd never felt any real attraction toward Zoe, physical or otherwise. It was true that back then, Natasha hadn't let herself think about Zoe that way, at least not consciously. But her body hadn't cared that Zoe was off limits. She'd tried her hardest to suppress those feelings.

It was true that the reason she and Zoe had gotten so close was because of their shared loneliness. Zoe, who felt like an outsider, and that no one understood her. Natasha, still trying to adjust to a world where Paige wasn't her whole life. Although that was what had brought them together, it wasn't the reason they'd fallen for each other. The feelings had been real. Otherwise, Natasha wouldn't still feel them now.

She should have known better than to speak so carelessly to Zoe. She had a heart like a butterfly, so delicate and difficult to hold on to without crushing it. Natasha had already hurt Zoe once, after all. It was at the top of her long list of regrets. Letting Zoe go wasn't what she regretted. How she'd done it, on the other hand? Natasha had regretted that for ten years.

She was still surprised that Zoe wasn't mad at her for what happened that night so long ago, when Zoe had turned up at her door. Natasha didn't want to revisit that night, but it was something they'd have to talk about eventually. She didn't know if telling Zoe the truth about it would make things worse or better between them.

But first, Natasha had to deal with the problems of the present. She rifled through her bag. She needed to call Zoe.

But when Natasha found her phone, she already had a text from her.

Can we meet up later? I want to talk.

Natasha shot a message back. *I was going to ask you the same thing.* She sent Zoe the name of a cafe, and they agreed to meet in half an hour.

She put down her phone and pulled her hair out of its ponytail. She ran her fingers through it. She was procrastinating. Contacting Zoe was only one of the things she had to address. That email from her mother was still in her inbox, unanswered.

Her parents. They were yet another of her regrets. If she hadn't made that fateful choice all those years ago, her life would have been very different from the one she was living now. Would it have been a better one? Natasha didn't know. All she knew is she'd had such a bright future ahead of her, and she'd given it all up.

If she could go back, would she do the same?

Natasha picked up her phone again and began to type out a response to her mother's email. It was just as formal as the email her mother had sent her. A polite greeting, followed by a stock line saying that, yes, she has been well. Natasha paused. All that was left was to answer the question of whether she wanted to meet with them.

But Natasha still didn't know the answer.

She slid her phone back into her bag and headed out to meet Zoe.

When Natasha arrived at the cafe, Zoe was already there,

sitting at a table in the corner nursing an enormous mug of coffee. Another cup, filled with steaming black coffee, sat on the table across from her.

Natasha took a seat and gave Zoe a muted smile. "Hi."

"Hey." Zoe nodded toward the coffee. "Still take it black?"

"Yes."

The weight of silence pressed down on them. Natasha hadn't actually thought about what to say to Zoe. She just wanted to apologize.

"Look," Zoe said. "I'm sorry. I overreacted. I've been such a mess since my physical therapist gave me the bad news. I was just feeling so raw and sensitive."

"I'm the one who should be apologizing," Natasha said. "I wasn't thinking. What I said was careless."

"No, you were right about everything. We were both lonely, and lost, and dealing with a lot. But even if it wasn't healthy, it doesn't mean it wasn't real. It meant a lot to me."

"It meant a lot to me, too." Natasha wrapped her hands around the warm coffee cup. "I've made so many mistakes in the past, but what you and I had wasn't one of them. And even though I didn't think about you 'that way,' it didn't mean there was no attraction there. I always held it back because you were off limits. But like you said, we don't have to worry about that anymore."

"So, we're good?" Zoe asked. "Because I really like spending time with you. I feel so lucky to have found you again. I don't want to lose that."

"You won't. We're okay."

Zoe smiled, but her smile was tinged with sadness.

"Is everything else all right?" Natasha asked.

"Yeah. I guess I'm still feeling kind of lost. Without dance, what do I have?" Zoe sighed. "I suppose there are advantages of not dancing anymore. No more shoving my feet into pointe shoes."

"No more mangled toes," Natasha said.

"No more spending hours straightening my hair so I can force it in a French twist."

"No more daily lessons." Even principal dancers still took lessons every day.

"No more constant aches and pains." Zoe rested her chin on her hand. "Who am I kidding? I'd do all of that every day until I died if it meant I could dance. Am I crazy?"

"No. Not at all."

"I mean, I left London because it was getting too hard to be immersed in the world of ballet when I couldn't be a part of it. I thought staying away would make things easier and give me some space to think." Zoe blew on her coffee, then took a sip. "But maybe running away from the thing that I love more than anything wasn't the best idea. And now that I know I'm not going to be able to dance for a while, maybe it's time I start looking into those alternatives you mentioned."

"Like teaching?" Natasha said.

"Maybe." Zoe sipped her coffee. "Lots of dancers go on to teach, so it seems logical. But I still don't know if it's something I'd enjoy."

"Why don't you come sit in on one of my classes? See what it's like?"

"I've been to enough ballet classes to know what they're like."

"But have you seen them from the other side? Or observed without taking part?"

"I guess not." Zoe's brows drew together. "That could be interesting."

"Then it's settled," Natasha said. "I have a class with the seniors next Monday. Why don't you come along? You can help me out too if you want."

"I don't know about that."

"I'm sure the class will be thrilled to have you there either way. A principal dancer in one of the most prestigious ballet companies in the world? You're a superstar to them."

"*Former* principal dancer." Zoe's eyes grew distant. "I guess now, I'll have to be something else."

"That's not a bad thing," Natasha said. "I've been thinking about a career change myself."

"Really? Don't you like teaching?"

"I do. But I've been at the same job, doing the same thing for years. It just doesn't satisfy me like it used to." She thought back to the unanswered email from her parents. "Perhaps it's time to move on."

12
ZOE

Zoe watched Natasha's students stretch. The class was all in their late teens. At that age, anyone who wasn't serious about ballet had given up long ago. Only those with talent and drive remained. These were the future soloists and principals. Zoe felt a pang of sadness. Their careers were only just beginning, while hers was ending.

Or maybe it was just changing.

She was keenly aware that half the students were staring and whispering about her. To them, Zoe was the closest thing to a rock star. She was used to the attention on stage and after performances, but outside of that, she still found it disconcerting.

Natasha clapped her hands together. "All right, let's get started."

There was a flurry of movement as the dancers scrambled about the room, spreading out along the barres.

"As you can see, we have a guest here tonight," Natasha said. "This is Zoe Waters, a principal dancer in the Royal London Ballet. And a former student of this academy."

It wasn't like everyone didn't know who Zoe was already. Nevertheless, murmurs went through the room.

"Zoe is going to help me teach the class tonight, so show her the same respect you would show me," Natasha said.

Zoe froze. She was going to help? She'd planned to just watch Natasha teach the class, not teach it herself. Zoe shot Natasha a look, but she had already begun the lesson, rattling off a list of warm-up exercises. The students sprung into motion.

Zoe walked over to Natasha and hissed in her ear. "What the hell? You're making me teach?"

"Yes." Natasha kept her eyes fixed on the class. "You wanted to know what teaching is like? What better way to learn about it than to do it yourself?"

"I don't know anything about teaching!"

"You've been taking classes for more than twenty years. You know more than enough to teach."

That was true. Ballet classes hadn't stopped once Zoe had gotten into a ballet company. All professional dancers still took daily classes on top of their rehearsals. "You could have at least warned me," she grumbled. "And since when did you become so spontaneous? What happened to 'there's a proper way to do things?'"

"You bring out my spontaneous side. Don't worry, I'll be right here with you helping." Natasha leaned closer and spoke to Zoe in a low, sultry voice. "I'll make it up to you afterward."

Blood rushed to Zoe's cheeks. Before she could ask what she meant, Natasha turned back to the class. "For now, we have a lesson to teach. Why don't you take over for a while? It's just barre work. It shouldn't be too difficult."

"Fine," Zoe said. This was the easiest part of the class. She might as well give it a try.

Natasha clapped her hands again, cutting off the music, and handed the class over to Zoe. Zoe led them through a series of exercises, then another, then another. Before she knew it, they'd run through a full set of barre work, and Natasha had barely gotten a word in.

"You're a natural at this," Natasha said. "Want to keep going?"

"Sure." Zoe wasn't about to admit it to Natasha, but she was enjoying herself. It was invigorating, being immersed in the world of ballet again. She felt only a shadow of the high she felt when she was the one dancing, but it was enough to remind her why she loved ballet in the first place.

"The class is yours." Natasha walked over to the side of the room and sat down on the bench. "I'll be over here if you need me."

The lesson ran for two hours, but time seemed to fly by. And Zoe found she was having fun. It was mostly because she decided to get creative with the class, coming up with unusual exercises just to spite Natasha, who always insisted on following conventions.

Zoe had the students leaping and pirouetting across the floor when Natasha announced that it was time for the lesson to come to an end. The students applauded and bowed or curtsied to Zoe, a ballet tradition that she'd always found strange, then began to gather their things and file out of the room. A few of them said bye to Zoe on the way out.

The studio emptied, but one student hung back. Natasha had addressed her by name earlier. Megan. She was tall and lanky, with skin a shade darker than Zoe's. She'd danced with confidence but became painfully shy whenever Zoe had addressed her.

Megan edged over to where Zoe stood. "Can I get a picture with you?"

Zoe smiled. "Sure."

Natasha stepped in, taking a picture of them with Megan's phone, before handing it back to her.

Megan hovered before them. "I have a poster of you on my wall," she blurted out. "From when you were in Swan Lake."

"Wow," Zoe said. "I'm flattered."

"You're the reason I'm still dancing. I've been taking ballet classes since I was little, but when I got old enough to start auditioning for schools, I kept getting knocked back. After so many rejections, I was ready to quit. Then, I saw a video of you dancing in Swan Lake." Megan let out a dreamy sigh. "You were incredible. It made me want to be just like you. So I kept at it. I have an audition for the New York Ballet coming up."

"I..." Zoe felt a flood of emotion. "That's amazing. You're going to ace that audition."

"Thanks." Megan beamed. "Are you going to teach the class again?"

Zoe glanced at Natasha. "I don't know. I'll think about it."

"Well, tonight was fun, so thanks." Megan waved goodbye and practically floated out of the room.

"Isn't that sweet?" Natasha said. "She really looks up to you."

Zoe screwed up her face. "I shouldn't be anyone's role

model. I don't know what I'm doing most of the time. I can't even keep my sister's houseplants alive."

"You don't need to know what you're doing. You just need to inspire people. And you did just that for Megan. You should be proud of yourself. Own it." Natasha wrapped her arms around Zoe's waist. "Wasn't that fun? Teaching might be a good fit for you."

Zoe scowled. "I still can't believe you sprang that on me."

"You did fine. I can't say I agree with your teaching style, but the students liked it."

"I believe you said you were going to make it up to me?"

Her hands still on Zoe's waist, Natasha took a few steps forward until their bodies were less than an inch apart. "I am."

Zoe crossed her arms between them. "And, how exactly are you going to do that?"

Natasha spoke into Zoe's ear. "By giving you a lesson of your own."

Zoe laughed. But the look on Natasha's face made her stop short. "You're serious?"

"I'm dead serious." Natasha drew a hand down Zoe's cheek. "Unless you'd rather your fantasies remain in your head?"

Heat curled up Zoe's neck. "No," she said. "I mean, yes. I want this. I want you."

"Then you're in luck." Natasha strolled over to the door, pulled it shut and twisted the lock. "That was the last class of the evening. Everyone should be gone by now. It's just the two of us."

Zoe's lips parted slightly. In the space of a few seconds, Natasha had transformed back into that icy, stern woman who had frustrated Zoe so much back when they'd started lessons together. But this Natasha had a playful glimmer in her eyes, and an insatiable desire that Zoe could feel across the room.

"So." Natasha wandered back over to where Zoe stood, holding her in place with her gaze. "What usually happened in these fantasies of yours?"

"Well," Zoe stammered. "We'd be having a lesson. And you'd just, grab my wrists."

Natasha's hands slithered down Zoe's forearms. She wrapped her fingers around Zoe's wrists. "Like this?"

"Yes."

"And then?"

Zoe's breath quickened. "And then, you'd push me up against the wall."

"Like this?"

Natasha backed Zoe into the wall, pinning her arms to it and pressing her body against her. The thick wooden barre dug into Zoe's lower back.

"Yes," Zoe whispered. "And then, you'd kiss me."

Natasha pressed her lips against Zoe's. Zoe crumbled, overcome by Natasha's passion. Zoe kissed her back, harder, channeling all her need into her lips.

Natasha released Zoe's wrists and glided her hands up Zoe's sides, cradling her curves through her skintight clothes. Zoe had dressed in a pair of dark tights and a long, form-fitting top, with a short wrap skirt around her hips. She wore nothing underneath, which was normal with dance clothes. Natasha's hand crept up to Zoe's breast. The other slid down to grab her ass cheek, pulling Zoe's hips into her own.

Zoe's head spun. Natasha was so intoxicating. The scent of her, a sweet fragrance with a hint of sweat from a day spent teaching. The taste of her soft, demanding lips. The press of her body, and the brush of her hair as it fell against Zoe's cheek.

Zoe reached for Natasha's hips, drawing her closer.

"Uh uh." Natasha broke away. "You were very specific about how this fantasy of yours went. If I remember correctly, it didn't involve you having the use of your hands. Hold on to the barre behind you."

Zoe obeyed, her heart racing.

"Hm. Something's missing." Natasha reached up to Zoe's head and untied the scarf wrapped around it, causing a few of her kinky curls to fall across her face. "This should work nicely."

Natasha tied the scarf around Zoe's wrist, wound it around the barre, and tied it to her other wrist. Zoe tugged at her bonds. They didn't budge. Her breath caught in her chest. Was this really happening?

Natasha took a few steps back and admired her handiwork. "There. Now, where were we?"

Natasha kissed her again, hard and deep. She slid a hand down the center of Zoe's stomach and flipped up her skirt, then ran her fingertips between Zoe's thighs. Her tights were already soaked through.

Natasha drew back. "I don't think I have to ask you what happens next."

Zoe trembled. Natasha snaked her hand under Zoe's skirt to grab the waistband of her tights. Slowly, she worked them down Zoe's hips, all the way to the ground. Zoe kicked them off her feet impatiently.

Once again, Natasha slipped her hand down to stroke Zoe's slit. She turned her head to peer at the mirror on the wall across from them, then whispered in Zoe's ear. "I want you to look in the mirror and watch us. I want you to see yourself as I do. See how mesmerizing I find you."

"Yes, Natasha," Zoe breathed.

Natasha fell to her knees, then pushed Zoe's thighs apart. "Don't close your eyes."

Zoe stared at the mirrored wall across from them. The sight of herself, disheveled and panting, with Natasha on her knees in front of her, only made her ache even more. She watched as Natasha skimmed her fingers up Zoe's legs, creeping higher and higher. Her head disappeared underneath Zoe's skirt. Anticipation sent blood rushing through her.

Finally, Natasha slipped her tongue between Zoe's lower lips. A sound between a whimper and a moan spilled from her mouth. Natasha grabbed Zoe's ass cheeks, pulling her in. Her fingertips dug into Zoe's skin.

"Oh, god," Zoe said. "Yes."

Natasha darted her tongue inside Zoe's entrance, a teasing motion that only made the thirst deep within her worse. She shifted her hips, desperate for more. In response, Natasha dragged her tongue up Zoe's throbbing clit, her grip on Zoe's cheeks tightening.

Zoe let out a low murmur. Her hands itched to grab hold of Natasha's head and pull her in harder, but she was powerless to do so. And it was so much more satisfying to surrender to Natasha's expert touch.

So Zoe leaned harder against the barre, her hands bound behind her. Resisting the urge to close her eyes, she watched them in the mirror. Natasha's head bobbing underneath her skirt. Herself, writhing against the wall, her chest rising and falling with her heavy breaths.

Natasha drew long, tight swirls around Zoe's bud with her tongue. A shiver of pleasure went through her. Zoe pushed her hips out greedily, trying to set off that explosion that was just outside her reach.

"Oh, yes!" Zoe cried. Pleasure erupted from deep in her core, spreading through her entire body. Her hands gripped the barre behind her as she struggled not to collapse. Natasha held Zoe's legs apart, working her tongue until Zoe shuddered and stilled.

Natasha unbound Zoe's wrists. Zoe slid down to the floor, her head rolling back against the wall. Natasha sat down next to her, her arms encircling her, and leaned in to plant a long, slow kiss on Zoe's lips.

"So," Natasha said. "How did that compare to those fantasies of yours?"

Zoe closed her eyes and sighed. "It was so much better."

What Zoe didn't tell Natasha was that those fantasies, no matter how wild, always ended with the two of them falling asleep in each other's arms. That was what she wanted more than anything.

13

ZOE

The day of the World Grand Prix had been the most nerve-wracking day of Zoe's life.

She'd waited anxiously in the corridor of the concert hall where the competition was being held, one earphone in her ear, playing a slow, calming song from one of her favorite classical ballets. She didn't have long until would be up on stage. She was trying so hard to center herself. But she couldn't stop thinking about the fact that this was her last chance to make the ballet world notice her.

Zoe looked at the clock on the wall. Soon, she'd have to go backstage with the rest of the contestants in her division. Almost everyone else was already gone.

But Zoe was waiting for Natasha.

She pulled out her phone. She'd sent Natasha a message ten minutes ago, asking where she was. Natasha had given Zoe her number for emergencies. This was as close to an emergency as things were going to get. But Natasha hadn't replied.

It was fine. She was probably on her way, driving so she

couldn't respond. But she was supposed to have come early so that the two of them could talk before Zoe's performance. Did she get lost on the way to the venue? Caught in traffic?

Natasha had to come. She'd promised Zoe she'd be here.

It wasn't like Zoe was alone. Dawn was back from her trip, and she was sitting in the audience, waiting for Zoe to perform. But right now, it was Natasha she wanted.

Zoe stretched her hamstring for the hundredth time. The familiar pre-performance anxiety was starting to set in, the kind that was neither good nor bad. All she had to do was channel it in the right direction, a feat which felt impossible right now.

The last of the stragglers headed backstage. Zoe couldn't stay here any longer. She picked up her bags and followed the others.

"Zoe?"

Zoe turned to see Natasha hurrying toward her. Relief washed over her. "You're here."

"I promised you I'd be here, didn't I?" Natasha said. "I wouldn't miss this for the world. I'm sorry I'm so late."

Zoe examined Natasha. She seemed a little frazzled. "Is everything okay?"

"Yes. Everything's fine."

"Are you sure?"

"Yes, it's nothing you need to worry about." Natasha clasped her hands together. "Now, it's time for you to go backstage, isn't it? Have you warmed up? Are you ready?"

"Yes," Zoe said. "But I don't feel ready. This is my last chance. What if I mess this up?"

"Zoe, stop. You're getting yourself all worked up."

"I can't help it! There's so much riding on this. My entire future is riding on this."

"Don't worry about that now," Natasha said. "You need to clear your head. You need to stop thinking, and feel. Just like you do in our lessons."

"This isn't a lesson. This is so much bigger than that." Zoe stared at her hands. They were shaking. Suddenly, the air felt stuffy and thick. "I've never been able to do well in competitions. I've never been able to dance as well on stage as I can in class."

"Zoe, look at me."

Zoe stared into Natasha's eyes. Those eyes of hers, which always conveyed more than her words ever did, were filled with a fierce determination.

"You need to forget about all those other times," Natasha said. "This time is going to be different. You've worked so hard the past few months. You've improved so much. You're not the same dancer you used to be."

Natasha took Zoe's hands in hers. They were warm and soft. Zoe's nerves began to dissipate, but her heart only beat even harder.

"I never say this enough. I never tell you how incredible, and talented, and special you are. I'm always correcting you and criticizing you, always trying to make you better and pushing you harder than I push any of my other students. It's because I know you have it in you. You have what it takes to make it. You can do this. I know you can."

"I can do this," Zoe echoed.

"When you're up there, on stage, just imagine you're back at the studio at the academy," Natasha said. "Pretend it's just the two of us, alone. And dance like you've danced for me so many times before. Let all your emotions shine through. Show everyone what it is that I see when you dance." Natasha's voice dropped to a whisper. "You're so beautiful when you dance for me."

Something flitted wildly inside Zoe's chest. Natasha still had hold of her hands, and Zoe never wanted to let go.

Behind her, someone cleared their throat. "Zoe Waters?" A man holding a clipboard was looking in their direction. "I'm looking for Zoe Waters, senior division."

Natasha released Zoe's hands. "She's right here."

"I should go," Zoe said.

"Don't forget what I said."

Zoe nodded. She headed backstage, without looking back, and took her place among the rest of the contestants. She soon found out she was performing fifth. That was a long time to stand around and wait. But it could have been worse.

The first dancer began her performance. As Zoe watched from the wings, she felt calm and ready. This was her last chance. She wasn't going to waste it. Especially not with Natasha watching.

It wasn't long until Zoe's name was called. She walked gracefully out onto the stage and got into position, waiting for the music to begin. She'd never attempted anything like this before, not with hundreds of people watching. The solo was complex, and she and Natasha had taken some artistic license with the choreography. Zoe needed to impress, after all. And if she could pull this off as well as she had in her lessons with Natasha, she would do just that.

As seconds passed, Zoe's calm began slipping away. She surveyed the crowd, looking for Natasha, but the hall was too big, and every seat was filled. She stopped searching. It didn't matter that she couldn't see Natasha. She knew Natasha was out there. She could do this.

Zoe took in a breath and closed her eyes. At once, she was back in the studio at the academy, alone with Natasha. When the opening notes of the haunting, ethereal tune rang out, she began to dance, not for the audience, but for the one person who mattered.

Zoe danced for Natasha as Aurora danced for her prince, in a magical vision conjured to charm him into falling in love with her. She cast a spell over the room, one that channeled everything she felt for Natasha. As Zoe danced, she realized something she'd been denying to herself. Natasha had captured her heart. And she wanted nothing more than to capture Natasha's heart in return.

The music rose. The tempo quickened. The melody transformed from solemn, to desperate, to hopeful. And Zoe leaped and twirled, dancing for her audience of one, barely aware of the gasps and murmurs coming from the crowd. Only Natasha mattered.

When the song ended, and Zoe came back down to earth, her pulse was pounding and her whole body was afire. It took her a few seconds to notice that the whole audience was standing. They were clapping and cheering as if they'd just witnessed a miracle.

Zoe looked out over the crowd, her smile wide and her eyes overflowing with tears of pride. As she curtsied for the third time, her eyes landed on Natasha, standing in the middle of the crowd. Natasha's smile told her one thing.

She had fallen under Zoe's spell.

Zoe headed toward the foyer, clutching her trophy in her hand. The competition had already ended, but she had spent the last hour backstage having her photo taken with the other winners. Now, she only had one thing on her mind. Finding Natasha.

Zoe made her way out into the foyer. It was almost empty now. She spotted Natasha standing to the side and called her name. Natasha turned toward Zoe, a wide smile on her face.

They met in the middle of the room and threw their arms around each other.

"You did it," Natasha said. "I'm so proud of you."

"I can't believe it." Zoe's head was still spinning. "I won. I actually won."

"I told you that you could do it. I always knew you had it in you. And today, everyone else got to see it too. I sat next to the artistic director of the Australian Ballet. You should have seen her face when you pulled off that perfect triple pirouette. There might be a job offer coming your way in the next few weeks."

"That would be amazing!" Zoe frowned. "But the Australian Ballet? They're on the other side of the world."

"Does it matter?"

"I guess not. I just haven't thought about the fact that I might have to move to another country."

"She wasn't the only one who was impressed," Natasha said. "You might end up with more than one option. Your mailbox is going to be filled with offer letters."

Zoe smiled. "You know, I don't think I could have done this without you here. Thank you. Really."

"I wouldn't have missed it," Natasha said. "And sorry again for being late."

"It's okay. All that matters is that you're here." Zoe thought back to their hurried conversation before her performance. "Is everything okay? You seemed worried earlier."

"I don't want to put a dampener on your win."

"It's okay. You can tell me."

"It's nothing," Natasha said. "Long story short, I ran into Paige again. But everything is fine. And that's enough about me. Today is about you."

"Right." Zoe couldn't help but wonder if there was more to what happened between Natasha and Paige than she let on. Every time Natasha mentioned her, there was something in her voice that spoke of some hidden pain. Natasha seemed sincere when she said they were over long ago. So why did Paige still unsettle Natasha like this?

Zoe shouldn't have cared in the first place. But she cared so much that it made her chest ache. She shouldn't have let her feelings for Natasha grow like this. She was Zoe's teacher. Zoe was her student. There were a thousand reasons why they could never be anything more.

But that didn't change the way Zoe felt about her.

"We should be celebrating your win," Natasha said. "You were incredible up there."

"Thanks." Warmth rose within Zoe's body. "It was all because of you."

"No, I had nothing to do with it. That wasn't anything I

taught you. I've seen you dance so many times now, but I've never seen you dance like that. Zoe, you were just magical."

"All I did was take your advice." Zoe reached for Natasha's hand and wrapped her fingers around it. "The entire time I was up there, I danced for you."

Zoe searched Natasha's eyes. Just like always, there was a storm brewing behind them, fierce and bright. But today, the passion in them had nothing to do with her love of dance.

Zoe's heart thumped against her ribs. There was no one else around now. She stepped in closer, until there were only inches between them, holding Natasha's gaze.

Natasha drew her hand up the side of Zoe's arm, desire radiating from her. Time seemed to stop, and the noise and motion of everything around them faded into nothing. The gap between their bodies grew smaller and smaller—

"Zoe!"

Zoe jerked back, releasing Natasha's hand, just in time to see her sister hurrying toward them.

"You were amazing up there!" Dawn wrapped her arms around Zoe tightly. "Congratulations! I'm so proud of you."

"Thanks." Zoe yanked herself away from her sister's smothering hug.

Silence hung in the air. Dawn seemed completely oblivious to what she'd just wandered into. Zoe glanced at Natasha. She looked calm and composed, as if nothing had even happened.

Zoe remembered herself. "Um, Dawn, this is Natasha. She's my teacher."

"Nice to meet you," Dawn said. "How kind of you to come support Zoe."

"It's no trouble," Natasha replied. "It's a pleasure. Zoe's one of my most talented students."

"I'm not surprised. She's come such a long way. It seems like just yesterday our little ballerina was going to class with her leotard on backward."

"That was one time!" Zoe said.

Dawn slipped her arm around Zoe's shoulder, squeezing her tight. "Are you ready? If you want a ride, we should get going."

Zoe looked at Natasha. "Actually, I'm getting a ride with Natasha."

"Okay. Just make sure you're home by dinner time. I'm sure Mom and Dad will want to celebrate your win." Dawn turned to address Natasha. "It was nice meeting you."

"You too," Natasha said.

As soon as Dawn was out of earshot, Natasha spoke. "I'm giving you a ride home, am I?"

"Yes." Zoe smiled sweetly. "I was thinking we could go get ice cream. It's our tradition after all."

"And when did *we* decide this?"

"Just now."

Natasha shook her head. "Okay. But I need to stop by my place first. It's on the way."

"That's fine with me."

"By the way, did you really go to class with your leotard on backward?"

"Only once." Zoe scowled. "Maybe twice. But I was six!"

Zoe followed Natasha toward the entrance. She was still feeling an incredible high, but it wasn't just from the win. There was one thing today had made her certain of.

She could no longer ignore her feelings for Natasha.

14

NATASHA

Natasha finished packing up the studio. It was Friday afternoon, and she was done with classes for the day. She grabbed her coat and slipped it on, then pulled her phone out of her pocket. She hadn't looked at it all day.

She frowned. Her mother had sent her another email. Natasha hadn't replied to her first email in the hope that ignoring it would make the problem would go away. Clearly, her mother wasn't giving up that easily.

Before Natasha had a chance to read it, a familiar figure strode through the door to the studio.

"Zoe," Natasha said. "What a lovely surprise."

"Just thought I'd stop by and say hi," Zoe said. "I just had a physical therapy session nearby."

"How was the session? Any improvement?"

"I've been given permission to do light exercise. I'm not going to be dancing en pointe any time soon, but it's better than nothing."

Natasha cupped Zoe's cheek. "That's wonderful."

"I'm in a pretty good mood now." Zoe draped her arms around Natasha's shoulders. "And I've decided I want to take you out on a date."

"Have you? I was starting to get the impression that you liked it when I wore the pants, so to speak."

Zoe grinned. "Only when it comes to certain things. Although, I do have selfish motives for this. There's something I want to do with you."

"What did you have in mind?"

"The Metro Ballet Company is performing *La Sylphide* tonight. Will you come see it with me?"

"Sure, if that's what you want." It hadn't been long since Zoe had burst into tears from just hearing the song from *Giselle*.

"It is. After teaching that class with you, I realized that ballet is in my soul. I miss it. I don't want to stay away anymore."

"Okay. Then we'll go to the ballet tonight." Natasha drew Zoe in and kissed her. Zoe melted into her, sending a surge of heat through her. Every time she kissed Zoe, it set her whole body alight.

"Natash- oh!"

Natasha broke away and looked toward the entrance to the studio. Julie, one of the other teachers, was standing in the doorway, her mouth hanging open.

"Julie," Natasha said.

"Sorry! I didn't mean to interrupt anything." Julie glanced at Zoe. Her eyes widened. "Zoe Waters? Is that you?"

"Yep." Zoe waved sheepishly. "Hi, Julie. It's been a while."

"I, uh, heard you were back in town."

"Yep. I'm just taking some time off."

Silence filled the room. Julie's eyes flicked between Natasha and Zoe.

Natasha cleared her throat. "Do you need something, Julie?"

Julie blinked. "I wanted to ask if you can take my Friday class next week. I have family visiting."

"Sure, no problem."

"Thanks. I'll get out of your hair." Julie glanced at Zoe again, then left the room.

"Oops," Zoe said. "Is it going to cause trouble for you?"

"No, it's fine," Natasha replied. "Although I would have chosen a less dramatic way to let everyone know we're dating." Julie wasn't exactly a gossip, but there was no way she'd keep what she saw to herself.

Zoe grimaced. "Sorry."

"Don't be. If I wanted to keep us a secret, I wouldn't have kissed you here in the studio." Natasha wasn't sure exactly what 'us' was. But she didn't want to think about something so complicated right now.

"Do you think anyone remembers that I used to be your student?"

"Who knows? Hopefully they won't be too scandalized when they figure it out." Of course, no one would suspect that there had ever been anything between Natasha and Zoe back then. Natasha wasn't usually the type to break the rules. But she was tired of playing by the rules. Perhaps that was Zoe rubbing off on her.

Zoe placed her hands on Natasha's waist and stepped in closer, smiling in that playful way of hers. "Well, if you really want to scandalize everyone…"

Natasha traced her hand up Zoe's bare arm. "As much as I don't care about who knows about us, there are far too many people in the building for a repeat of the other evening." She lowered her voice. "And we'll have plenty of time for that later tonight."

"I'm going to hold you to that."

The honeyed warmth in Zoe's voice sent a thrill up Natasha's spine. "We should both go home and get ready. I'll see you in a couple of hours."

After a quick dinner at a cozy little restaurant of Zoe's choosing, Natasha and Zoe made their way to the concert hall where they'd gone on their first date. They reached it with minutes to spare. As they slipped into their seats, the lights went out and the show began.

Natasha relaxed in her seat and let herself get lost in the story. *La Sylphide* was a classic romantic ballet about a man who fell in love with a sylph, a spirit of the air. Natasha had always found it ironic that most 'romantic' ballets ended in tragedy. But still, she enjoyed the way they portrayed love as this pure, beautiful thing that had the power to transcend even death.

Natasha glanced at Zoe. She was on the edge of her seat, a faraway look in her eyes. As Natasha watched her, she felt familiar feelings building inside. A yearning in her chest that was almost painful. A longing that went beyond simple desire. The certainty that she would move mountains for this woman, just to see her smile.

Natasha hadn't often felt like this before in her life. After

Paige, she'd been slow to open up her heart to anyone. She'd given everything to Paige, given up everything for her, but Paige had been careless with Natasha's heart. So, she'd kept her heart closed, for fear of giving it to the wrong person again. Could Zoe be the right person? Despite how everything between them had started, nothing about this felt wrong.

Natasha turned her eyes back to the stage. She soon found herself engrossed in the comfortingly familiar story once again. When the show ended, she felt like only minutes had passed.

Once the applause died down and the lights went up, Natasha and Zoe joined the crowd that was streaming out of the hall, chatting about the show as they walked. It was Zoe who did all the talking. All night, she'd been full of that uncontainable excitement that Natasha had always found so charming. Natasha was glad that this part of Zoe still existed. Zoe had been so down about everything since they reconnected. Her happiness was contagious.

When they reached the foyer, Zoe broke off. "I'm going to run to the ladies' room. I'll be right back."

"I'll wait here," Natasha said.

Zoe disappeared into the tightly packed crowd. A few minutes passed. As Natasha waited, she remembered the email her mother had sent her earlier. She hadn't opened it yet. She pulled out her phone and skimmed through the email. Her parents were here in the city now, and they were planning to stay for five more days. The message ended with Natasha's mother's cell phone number and a request that Natasha call her as soon as possible.

Natasha stared at her phone. She could ignore this email,

just as she had the last one, but her mother's persistence gave her pause. She had to make a decision. It shouldn't have been this hard. But Natasha had never been good at making decisions. She was always afraid of making the wrong choice. What if she gave her parents a chance, and they rejected her again? What if she put it all on the line, and she just ended up getting hurt?

She put her phone away. Zoe had been gone for a while now, and the restrooms weren't far. Natasha edged through the crowd and headed off in search of Zoe.

She went down a corridor and rounded a corner. A few feet away stood a small cluster of people. Zoe was right in the middle of them, having her picture taken with a trio of teenage girls who had the distinctive look of ballet dancers.

Natasha crossed her arms and leaned back against the wall, watching with amusement. So these were fans of hers. As much as Zoe claimed to be unused to her fame, it didn't show. She was a natural, lighting up the space around her and everyone in it. Natasha wasn't surprised. Zoe had always been a star in her eyes.

As she looked on, all those feelings stirred inside her again. She could trust Zoe to take care of her heart. Somehow, she just knew it. But could Natasha be trusted with Zoe's? She'd already hurt Zoe once before, and she still hadn't made it right. She still hadn't told Zoe the truth about that night. It was a night she didn't want to relive.

At least, that was what Natasha told herself. There was also the fact that the truth could end up hurting Zoe even more. Natasha just didn't want to risk hurting Zoe a second time. And she was afraid of revealing to Zoe how weak she had been to end up in that situation in the first place.

As the last of the people around Zoe dispersed, she spotted Natasha and hurried over.

"Done with your adoring fans?" Natasha teased.

"Yeah," Zoe replied. "Sorry for keeping you waiting. That always happens when I go somewhere that there are lots of ballet lovers. It's been a while. I forgot all about it."

"It's fine." Only Zoe could forget that she was a star. "Does it bother you? The fans I mean?"

"Not really. It's just still weird. And a few of them asked me about when I'm going to return to the stage. I didn't know what to tell them. I still haven't figured out what to do next."

"You have plenty of time to figure it out." Natasha slipped her arm around Zoe's waist. "But we have a very important decision to make right now."

"What's that?"

"Your place or mine?"

Zoe smiled. "How about yours? I haven't seen it yet."

That wasn't true. Zoe had been to Natasha's house once, although she hadn't been inside. It was the last night they saw each other ten years ago.

Natasha pushed the thought out of her mind. "Mine it is."

15
ZOE

Zoe looked around the living room. It was exactly what she'd expected of Natasha's home. Everything was dark, rich and spacious. Classical music echoed through the room from hidden speakers. Right now, a song from Swan Lake was playing.

The conversation lapsed into silence. Zoe let out a contented murmur, taking everything in. They'd been sitting in the living room talking and drinking wine for what felt like hours. It was the perfect end to the perfect night.

"Tonight was amazing," she said. "Thanks for coming along with me."

"Thanks for taking me," Natasha replied. "So you had a nice time?"

"Yeah. It was a little bittersweet, watching everything from the outside. But even if I can't be on stage, even if I can't dance, I still want to be a part of this world."

"Any ideas about what you're going to do yet?"

"Not really." A few days ago, Zoe had spoken with the director of The Royal London Ballet about her future. He said they'd love to have her back with the company in some way, even if she couldn't dance. But that would mean moving back to London, and away from Natasha again.

She sighed wistfully. "I wish you'd been able to watch me dance. Just once. I've come a long way in ten years."

"I wish I had too," Natasha said. "You have no idea how many times I almost got on a plane to go see one of your performances."

"Why didn't you?"

"I was afraid we'd run into each other."

"Would that have been such a bad thing?" Zoe asked.

"Not bad. Just… difficult. As time went on, the distance between us just got bigger and bigger until it felt impossible to overcome."

"I felt that too," Zoe said. "I never thought I'd see you again. But here we are."

"Here we are." Natasha took Zoe's hand in hers. "Still, I would have loved to see your Giselle. That role was made for you. It's so full of emotion."

"I can show you," Zoe said. "Right now."

"Here?"

"Why not?"

"What about your ankle?" Natasha asked.

"Natasha. Stop worrying. Let me dance for you. I want to."

"Okay." Natasha released Zoe's hand. "Dance for me."

Zoe stood up and walked across the living room to where the rug gave way to bare wooden floorboards. "Do you have the music?"

"Of course." Natasha picked up her phone and paused the song that was playing. "What do you want to show me?"

"Giselle's solo from the first act." It was when Giselle first fell in love with her suitor, before his betrayal, and her heartbreak and death. Back when everything was simple and happy.

Zoe got into position. Natasha pressed play. The song began.

And Zoe danced.

It was just like that final night on stage, when she'd danced that impossibly perfect performance. But this time, she didn't have to pretend Natasha was watching her. This time, Natasha was really there. It wasn't the real piece, of course. Zoe danced on a tiny stage bounded by the rug and the wall behind her, barefoot instead of en pointe, with an injured ankle and after a few glasses of wine. But the passion was there. The meaning was there. And the intensity of what she felt for Natasha showed through in every step.

Zoe lost herself in the music, and in her audience of one, holding Natasha captive with the motions of her body. As the piece rose to a crescendo, she pirouetted across the floor in a flurry of turns, letting the swelling music carry her. The world spun, and she spun with it—

—until the last turn brought her right into Natasha's waiting arms.

Before Zoe had a chance to steady herself, Natasha pulled her in close. She drew the pad of her thumb across Zoe's lower lip. "You're so beautiful when you dance for me."

Natasha kissed her, soft and slow. At once, Zoe came

apart. Their tongues and lips danced around each other, their arms intertwining. She felt like she was in a dream. The wine, the sensations, Natasha herself—it all made her head spin and her body feel weightless.

When Zoe came up for air, Natasha continued to kiss her, below her ear, then down the side of her neck, all the way to the base of her throat. She tugged down the front of Zoe's dress, freeing her breasts so she could kiss the slight contours they formed. She took one of Zoe's nipples in her mouth, rolling her tongue back and forth over it. Zoe let out a heavy breath. Natasha took the other nipple and sucked it, first gently, then harder through her teeth.

Zoe cried out, writhing against the wall. Natasha lavished attention on her breasts, licking, sucking, and biting until Zoe ached with need. Sensing her arousal, Natasha pushed her hand down to cup Zoe between her thighs, grinding her palm into her through her dress. Zoe wished for nothing more than for all those layers of fabric between the two of them to disappear.

"Natasha," she begged.

Zoe didn't have to say anything more. Natasha pulled her toward the bedroom in a whirlwind of passion, bumping into the doorframes and tables on the way. Once they reached it, Natasha pulled Zoe's dress over her head, then pushed her down onto the bed. Her gaze slipped along Zoe's body. The lust in her dark eyes made Zoe crave her even more.

Natasha stripped off her own dress. Underneath, she wore a matching set of lacy midnight blue lingerie. Zoe drank her in with her eyes. Natasha had once said that she had the 'wrong' body for ballet. There was nothing wrong about Natasha's body. It was perfect in every way. It was like a dancer's in some ways, lean and toned, but Natasha had more curves and an inviting softness.

Natasha didn't give Zoe much of a chance to admire her. She leaned down and stripped Zoe's panties from her legs, then took off her own bra and panties, dropping them to the floor behind her. Natasha climbed onto the bed and swooped down to kiss Zoe again. Their bodies ground against each other, their arms and legs entangling, dancing a sensual pas de deux to music only they could hear.

Zoe felt the heat of Natasha's arousal on her thigh and slipped her hand down between the other woman's legs. Her slit was warm and slick. She drew her fingers up Natasha's folds, tracing the outlines of her inner lips, feeling each petal they formed. Her fingertip reached Natasha's hard, pink nub. Zoe skimmed her finger over it, eliciting a shiver from the other woman.

Natasha grabbed Zoe's wrist and pushed it down to the bed next to her. "Wait right there." She crawled off the bed and opened the bottom drawer of the nightstand next to it.

Zoe rolled onto her side to peek into the drawer, but she found herself distracted by Natasha's naked figure. Her smooth, pearl-white skin. Her full breasts, which looked like their tips had been painted the palest of pinks. Her hair, falling down like a sheet on either side of her face as she leaned over. Zoe had never seen anything more beautiful.

Natasha straightened up. There was a strapless strap-on in her hand, a curved, double ended dildo that was pink and smooth, with slight bumps and ridges. It looked more like some kind of abstract sculpture than anything obscene. Natasha placed it on the bed and climbed back onto it.

Zoe lay back, burning with anticipation. Natasha nudged Zoe's legs apart and kneeled between them. She dipped down to kiss Zoe's stomach, drawing her free hand down Zoe's side as she kissed lower and lower, past her belly button, all the way to the peak of Zoe's lower lips. She parted them with her fingers and kissed down Zoe's slit, her lips fluttering against Zoe's swollen bud. The throbbing deep below grew unbearable.

Natasha darted her tongue out to lick Zoe's folds. She swirled it around Zoe's entrance. It only made Zoe hunger for what was coming even more.

Natasha straightened up. "Are you ready?"

"I've always been ready for you," Zoe said.

Natasha picked up the toy from the bed. It had two ends, one short and hooked, the other long and straight. Natasha parted Zoe's lips and pushed the short end inside.

At once, Zoe felt a satisfying fullness that quickly transformed into a desperate ache. She looked down at herself. The short end was deep inside her, but the long end stood up almost vertically. Natasha threw one leg over her, kneeling above Zoe's hips. She grabbed the long end of the strapless toy and positioned herself above it. Then she lowered herself onto Zoe slowly.

Zoe gasped. The weight of Natasha's body made the end of the toy that was inside Zoe jolt and move in the most exquisite way. She wriggled her hips experimentally. More darts of pleasure went through her. Judging by the shudder that went through Natasha's body, the same thing was happening on her end.

Natasha placed a hand between Zoe's breasts. "Slowly now."

Natasha began to move her hips, not up and down, but back and forth, rocking and grinding. Zoe let out a long moan. Every motion Natasha made reverberated through her, so Natasha's ecstasy echoed her own. Zoe matched her movements, rolling her hips, feeling Natasha inside her and herself inside Natasha.

Natasha reached up to anchor herself on the headboard with one hand, the other massaging Zoe's breasts and nipples. Zoe grabbed hold of Natasha's waist, her whole body rising up to meet her with every thrust. She trembled feverishly.

"Are you close?" Natasha asked.

"Yes."

"Come with me."

Zoe whimpered. She couldn't keep herself from coming apart for much longer. And as Natasha ground harder and faster, the pressure inside her rose and rose uncontrollably.

But it was Natasha who came first. Her body quaked, her lips forming a wide "O" in a silent scream. The sight of Natasha atop her, mouth open in orgasmic bliss, pushed Zoe over the edge. She arched up from the bed as her pleasure reached a crescendo, spreading from deep in her core to flood every cell in her body. Zoe clutched onto Natasha, who was still riding the throes of her own orgasm, until both of them collapsed onto the bed.

When Zoe returned to her body, she found Natasha next to her, her eyes closed, her arms draped possessively around Zoe's body. Zoe nestled in closer. Wasn't this what she'd always dreamed of? Falling asleep in Natasha's arms?

As she lay there, Zoe realized something she'd been hesitant to admit.

She couldn't go back to London. Not if it meant being apart from Natasha again.

16

NATASHA

*N*atasha would never forget the moment everything changed between herself and Zoe.

It had been a Tuesday afternoon, a few weeks after Zoe's win at the World Grand Prix. Natasha had just finished one of her group classes when Zoe had shown up at her studio without warning.

She was fielding questions from a couple of students who had stuck around after class, so she could do no more than shoot Zoe a questioning glance. But Zoe gave nothing away. She just stood by the door patiently.

What was going on? They'd had a private class the evening before, and Zoe had been fine. She hoped everything was okay. Natasha had become invested in her star student. She wanted Zoe to succeed.

No, Natasha was far more than invested. And Natasha didn't just *want* Zoe to succeed. She *needed* Zoe to succeed, more than she needed anything else. Zoe's happiness and her own were inextricably linked. It wasn't normal to feel this way about a student. But nothing about what was between the two of them was normal.

Natasha finished off her conversation with her students and walked them to the door. As soon as they were gone, she turned to Zoe. "What's going on?"

"I got a phone call." Zoe's voice was as blank as her expression. "Just an hour ago."

"From who?" Natasha asked.

"The Director of The Royal London Ballet. He called me himself."

"And? What did he say?"

"And they offered me a position."

"Zoe, that's incredible!"

"I'm going to be a professional dancer." A smile spread across Zoe's face. "And at one of the top ballet companies in the world! I'll be in the corps, of course. But the director, he said I have talent, and they'll be keeping an eye on me. Maybe I'll become a soloist one day. Or even a principal." She shook her head. "I still can't believe it."

"I can believe it," Natasha said. "I always knew you had it in you."

"I couldn't have done it without you. I can't even begin to thank you for everything you've done."

"I didn't do anything. And you don't have to thank me. Seeing you succeed is enough of a reward."

"Well, thank you anyway." Zoe threw her arms around Natasha's neck and pulled her in for a hug.

Natasha's heart sped up. The two of them were all alone. After a moment's hesitation, she wrapped her arms around Zoe in return. Zoe's body felt warm against hers. Her skin was like velvet. As the embrace stretched out, Natasha knew she should let go. She shouldn't be seen with a student like this.

But she didn't care.

Natasha pulled back slightly, but didn't release Zoe from her arms. Zoe's dark eyes searched hers. They were filled with the same longing Natasha felt deep within herself.

"Natasha," Zoe said softly.

Natasha didn't remember how exactly it happened. All she knew was that one moment, the two of them were standing there, arms around each other. Then the next, her lips were on Zoe's, and Zoe's lips were on hers, in an urgent, fiery kiss.

Natasha closed her eyes. Zoe's hand slid up the side of Natasha's neck and behind her head, her fingers threading through Natasha's hair. Natasha grabbed onto Zoe's waist, drawing her closer. She lost herself in Zoe's lips, and her body, and the sheer desire that threatened to consume them both.

Why had she ever resisted this? *How* had she ever resisted this? Zoe was so intoxicating. The heat that smoldered between them was like nothing she'd had ever felt before.

But Natasha knew it was wrong.

She tore herself away. "That was—" She shook her head. "I shouldn't have done that."

"No, it was me," Zoe said. "And why not? Natasha, we've been dancing around these feelings for so long now."

"This isn't a good idea."

"Why not?"

Natasha threw her hands up. "For a dozen reasons. For starters, you're my student."

"Not for much longer."

"You're my former student. Somehow, I don't think anyone who could walk in here and see us would make the distinction. Neither would the director of the academy."

"Then let's go somewhere else," Zoe said.

"No. It's still inappropriate. You're ten years younger than me."

"Does it matter? We're both adults."

"Yes, it matters!" Natasha folded her arms across her chest. "And even if it didn't, you're moving to the other side of the world."

"Not for a couple more weeks," Zoe said. "And we can figure something out."

"No, we can't. Zoe, think about your career. What do you think would happen if news got out that there was something going on between you and your teacher?"

"We can keep it a secret."

"No, we can't." Natasha rubbed at her forehead. "I've been down that road, and it's not an easy one."

"Then we won't keep it a secret," Zoe said. "Who cares what anyone thinks?"

"You don't mean that. And I wouldn't let you do that to your career."

"It would be my choice."

"Zoe." Natasha brought her hand up to her forehead. "Just, sit down with me."

Natasha waited for Zoe to sit on the bench, then sat down next to her, careful to leave a space between them. She should never have let things get this far. She should never have let herself get this close to a student. It would be a kindness to Zoe to end this as definitively as possible. To tell her on no uncertain terms that nothing could ever happen between them.

But when she looked at Zoe, she lost her resolve. She couldn't hurt Zoe like that. Natasha had to let her down easy.

Natasha folded her hands in her lap. "Zoe, you know this can never be."

"No, I don't," Zoe said. "All the reasons you've given me make it difficult, but not impossible."

"Please, just forget all that for a moment. You just got accepted into one of the top ballet companies in the world. You're about to start a new life in London. You're at the beginning of this incredible journey that will take you to places you've only dreamed of. You can't do all that while you're still holding onto attachments from the past. You don't need any distractions."

"You're not an attachment. Or a distraction. You're the reason I have the chance to live my dreams in the first place."

"You know how hard being a professional dancer is," Natasha said. "There's no way to make something like this work when we're on opposite sides of the globe."

"But…" Slowly, Zoe's face fell. Her shoulders slumped forward. "You're right. I know you're right. It was silly of me to even think about it."

"It wasn't silly. But there's a whole world out there waiting for you. You need to be free to go out there and find your place in it."

"But if everything was different?" Zoe gazed back at Natasha. "Do you think we could ever…"

"Maybe. But there's no point dwelling on things that can

never happen."

"I guess you're right."

Natasha hesitated, then patted Zoe on the hand. "I have some time before my next class. Why don't we go celebrate? It is our tradition, after all."

Zoe smiled faintly. "Okay. Let's go."

As they left the studio, Natasha couldn't help but wonder if Zoe had really accepted that there could never be anything between them.

17

NATASHA

Natasha was in the kitchen making pancakes when Zoe wandered out of the bedroom. She was wearing nothing but her panties and an oversized white t-shirt of Natasha's, her long, brown legs poking out the bottom. Natasha didn't know where Zoe had found the shirt, but she wasn't complaining. She'd never seen anyone look so enchanting in a t-shirt.

"Morning," Zoe said.

"Good morning." Natasha lifted the pancake out of the pan and added it to the growing stack on the plate next to the stove. She'd almost burned it because she was staring at Zoe. "Look who's finally awake."

"Finally? What time is it?"

"10:30." Natasha took Zoe by the waist and kissed her gently. "Your timing is perfect. These pancakes are just about finished. I hope you're hungry."

"I did work up quite an appetite after last night." Zoe leaned down on the counter next to her. "But I could stand to work up even more of one right now."

"Nice try. After breakfast." Natasha tipped her head toward the dining table. "Go sit down."

"Yes, ma'am."

"Don't you dare call me ma'am. I don't need another reminder that I'm pushing forty."

Zoe sat down at the table and rested her chin on her hands. "Last night was amazing. And you fulfilled another one of my fantasies."

"Oh? And what was that?"

"Falling asleep in your arms."

Natasha brought the pancakes over to the table and planted a kiss on Zoe's cheek. "I liked that part too."

Natasha sat down. Zoe smothered her pancakes with maple syrup and took a bite.

"Mm," she said. "I have to admit, I was a little disappointed I woke up alone. But this makes up for it."

"Next time we can wake up together and make breakfast together too," Natasha said.

"Next time?"

"Yes. Just as long as you wake up at a reasonable hour."

"I'll try my best." Zoe smiled. "So, I've been thinking. I've been sulking about my career ending for too long. It's time to start seriously looking into my options. Into the future."

"That's great. What were you thinking?"

"Well, the Royal London Ballet said I could come back and work for them." She looked up from her plate at Natasha. "But I was thinking of looking for a job here in the States. Hopefully here in the city."

Natasha put her fork down. "You want to stay here?"

"Well, yeah. There are plenty of job opportunities. I've made lots of contacts in the ballet community over the years, and I know a few people who live here. It wouldn't be hard for me to find a job of some kind. Besides, we have something special here, don't you think? I wouldn't want to lose that. Not again."

"I don't want to lose that either. But I don't like the idea of you staying here just for me."

"Things are different this time. I wouldn't be sacrificing anything. And Natasha, we've finally found each other again after ten years. You're crazy if you think I'm going to up and leave again." Zoe paused. "Unless you don't want me to stay."

"Of course I do. As long as it's what you want."

"It is what I want. And that's what I'm going to do." Zoe picked up the jug of maple syrup, poured even more on her pancakes, and continued with her breakfast.

As the conversation moved to more mundane topics, Natasha wondered what it would be like to do this every morning. To wake up with Zoe in her bed, to eat breakfast together, to spend the day lazing around, doing nothing at all. It sounded so utterly normal. But Natasha wanted nothing more.

Midway through breakfast, Natasha's phone rang. The call was from an unknown number. She groaned. "I should take this. It's probably one of my students' overbearing mothers. Some of them don't understand the concept of boundaries."

"Go ahead," Zoe said.

Natasha picked up the phone. "Hello?"

"Natasha? Is that you?"

Natasha froze. It had been a long time since she'd heard

that voice, but she recognized it instantly. "Mom? How did you get my number?"

"I called your work yesterday and asked for it. I just said I'm your mother, and it's important that I get in touch with you."

Natasha scowled. She was going to have to have a word with the receptionist. "What is it?"

"Did you get my emails?" her mother asked.

"Yes."

"Oh. It's just that, you didn't reply."

Natasha ignored the hurt in her mother's voice. Her mother had always been good at making Natasha seem like the unreasonable one.

"Well then, you'll already know what this is about," her mother said. "Your father and I are in the city for a few more days. We'd love to have dinner with you."

Was her mother seriously pretending they hadn't spoken at all for the past twenty years? Natasha almost hung up. But there was something about her mother's tone that gave her pause.

"Why?" Natasha asked. "Why now?"

"It's not something I want to explain on the phone." Her mother said. "But it's important that you meet us."

Please. That was what her mother was trying to say. But she was too proud to actually say it. She hadn't changed one bit.

Nevertheless, Natasha felt a pang of guilt. "Fine. Pick a time and a place, and send me the details. I'll be there."

Natasha hung up the phone without saying goodbye.

"Everything okay?" Zoe asked.

"That was my mother." Natasha began attacking what

remained of her breakfast, cutting up her pancakes with a furiousness that startled even herself. "I'm sure you figured that out already."

"I'm guessing you and your parents are still on bad terms?"

"Yes. It's been twenty years since I last saw them. But they're in town, and they want to meet up for dinner. I've been ignoring my mother's emails. All it took for me to fold was a phone call."

"For you to fold?" Zoe said. "Giving your parents a chance isn't a sign of weakness."

"Isn't it? I'm almost forty. I'm a grown woman with my own life, but apparently, I still want my parents' approval. If that isn't weakness, I don't know what is."

"Stop beating yourself up." Zoe reached across the table and put her hand on Natasha's. "They're your parents. You're allowed to want their approval. And you don't have to meet with them if you don't want to. But if you do, that's okay too."

"I don't know. Something tells me I should do this. They're getting older. Maybe I should give them a chance before it's too late." Natasha sighed. "At least we'll be in public, so they have to be relatively civil." If her parents hadn't changed since Natasha last saw them, getting into a yelling match was a real possibility.

"Well, if you need backup, I can come along," Zoe said. "It might make things easier."

Natasha examined Zoe thoughtfully. "That's not a bad idea. If there's someone else there, my parents will really have to play nice." Plus, although she didn't say it out loud, she could use the support. "Are you sure you want to come?"

"I'm happy to," Zoe said. "You've been there for me so many times. Now I can return the favor."

"Thanks. I really appreciate it."

Zoe smiled. "No problem."

It took a few moments for Natasha to realize what she'd done.

She'd just invited Zoe to meet her parents.

18
ZOE

On the day of Zoe's last class with Natasha, she'd headed into the academy building, weighed down by the knowledge that this was the last time she'd see her teacher. Since getting the offer from the Royal London Ballet, Zoe had no reason to continue taking lessons in the first place. She'd dropped her group classes, but she'd continued with her lessons with Natasha just to stay in shape.

At least, that was what she'd told herself. In truth, it was because she didn't feel ready to move on. From the academy. From the city she'd lived in her entire life. From her family.

From Natasha.

Zoe entered the studio. Natasha was already there. She stood by the barre, a cloudy expression on her face.

"Zoe." Natasha pointed to the bench next to her. "Sit down. *Now.*"

Zoe did as she was told, her stomach churning. She already had an idea of what this was about.

Natasha walked over to the doors and pushed them shut, then returned to stand in front of Zoe, her hands on her hips. "Have you accepted the Royal London Ballet's offer?"

"Yes." Zoe had accepted it, but she hadn't signed anything yet. It wasn't too late for her to back out.

"That's funny. Because I just heard that you were offered a position with Riverside Ballet, and you told them that you'd consider it."

Crap. Riverside Ballet was a small local ballet company. Word traveled fast around here.

"Is it true?" Natasha asked.

Zoe lowered her head to stare at her lap. "Yes."

Natasha recoiled. "What the hell, Zoe? Why would you tell them something like that?"

"I…" Zoe bit her lip. "I don't know."

"You don't know?" Natasha's voice rose. "So you have no explanation as to why you're thinking about throwing away the opportunity of a lifetime? The very thing we've been working toward for months now? That you've been working your entire life for?"

Zoe looked up at Natasha. She'd never seen her like this before. Zoe had seen her frustrated, and irritated, even disappointed. But she'd never seen Natasha angry.

"Zoe, this is the Royal London Ballet, for gods' sake! You are *not* turning down their offer."

"But—" Zoe's voice quivered.

"But what?"

"I don't want to move to London."

"Are you serious?" Natasha's voice echoed through the studio. "That's what this is about? You're afraid of moving away from home?"

"It's not just that. It's the people that I'll be leaving behind." Zoe's fingers curled in her lap. "Like you."

Their eyes locked. The fury in Natasha's gaze faded slightly.

Natasha looked away. "Zoe, this is your dream. You can't throw everything away for someone else."

"I'm not throwing anything away. I'll still have a job with a ballet company, just not the Royal London Ballet. If I take the position with Riverside—"

"No." Natasha began to pace in front of her. "That's not an option. You're far too talented to dance for some small no-name ballet company."

"But I'll still be living my dream," Zoe said. "Doing what I love. Isn't that what matters?"

"Your dreams are so much bigger than this. We both know you belong on center stage."

"But if I join a smaller company, it'll be far easier for me to become a soloist. Or even a principal."

"When I say center stage, I'm talking about the world stage." Natasha sat down next to her. "Isn't that what you said you wanted? To earn your place at the top? To show the world what you're capable of?"

"That was just childish nonsense. I don't care about any of that. I care about you."

"You need to forget about me. You should be thinking about what's best for you."

"Forget about you? I couldn't do that if I tried."

Natasha sighed. "I can't let you make a mistake like this. I know how you feel. I really do. I've been where you are. And I don't want you to throw your life away for someone else like I did."

"Like you did?" Zoe asked. "What do you mean?"

Natasha was silent. Zoe could see the battle going on behind her eyes. What was it about this that she was finding so hard?

Finally, Natasha spoke. "When I was eighteen, I was faced with a choice between love and my own ambitions, and I made the wrong one. I chose love. And I've regretted it ever since."

"When you were eighteen? Do you mean Paige?"

Natasha nodded.

"What happened?"

"It's a long story. Do you really want to hear it?"

"I do."

Natasha didn't say anything at first. Then she leaned back and crossed her ankles, her eyes fixing on something across the room. "Paige and I, we have a long, complicated history. We met in ballet class when I was nine. From that day on, we were inseparable. For most of my childhood, she was my best friend. And as we got older, we became more than friends. But back then, it was impossible for two girls to be together. That didn't stop us from trying. Paige's parents were determined to turn a blind eye to what was going on between us. But my parents reacted differently. I'd always thought we had a good relationship, but when they found out about me and Paige, they refused to accept it. They did their best to keep me from her, but it didn't work. We still found ways to be together.

"Both of us dreamed of a life where we could be free from everyone and everything that tried to keep us apart," Natasha said. "By the time we were in twelfth grade, Paige had already started auditioning for ballet companies. Me, I'd given up on ballet. But I had talents other than dance. I'd always been interested in journalism, so I focused on my studies so I could get into a college with a good journalism program. In the end, I managed to get a full ride scholarship for one of the best colleges in the country. Not that I needed it. My parents had enough money to fund my education, no matter where I chose to go. But it shows how much potential I had. My future was filled with opportunity. The world had opened up. And it excited me."

That was exactly how Zoe had felt when she'd gotten that job offer from the Royal London Ballet. At least, until she'd realized it meant leaving Natasha.

"But I couldn't bear the thought of being apart from Paige," Natasha said. "And when she got an offer from the Metro Ballet Company, she took it. It was too good an opportunity to pass up. But it meant she'd have to move away. We talked about it, and she asked if I'd move with her. It was our chance to finally be together freely, away from our parents. That's what she promised me. That we would be together openly.

"Naively, I believed her. I was in love with her, after all. So I followed my heart. I agreed to move here with her. I applied for college here, and I was accepted, but when I told my parents about it, they were furious. They told me that they wouldn't fund my education if I ran off with Paige. They said they'd cut me off."

Zoe's heart sank. Natasha had mentioned before that she and her parents didn't talk anymore, but she hadn't gone into detail. Zoe couldn't imagine what that was like. Despite all Zoe's problems, at least her family supported her no matter what.

"At the time, I didn't believe they'd actually do it," Natasha said. "Apart from everything with Paige, we'd always been so close. I thought they were bluffing. And even if they weren't, I wasn't going to let them stand in the way of true love. So I left my old life behind and followed Paige here.

"As it turned out, my parents weren't bluffing. They cut me off completely. I had to give up on college and get a reception job here at the academy to make ends meet, and I eventually ended up with a teaching position. It wasn't what I planned, but it worked. And I had Paige. She was all I needed."

Zoe studied Natasha's face from the side. Despite her impassive expression, there was a hint of wistfulness in her eyes.

"It was great at first," Natasha said. "But Paige insisted we keep our relationship secret because she thought it would affect her career. Back then, that kind of thing was still a big deal, even in the ballet world. At least, it was for women. She was worried about her image. She promised me that as soon as she established herself as a dancer, then we could be together openly. Just as soon as she made it out of the corps. Just as soon as she got through this next production. Just as soon as she made principal dancer.

"Well, eventually, she did become a principal. And nothing changed. It took me years to realize nothing was ever going to change. Her career would always come before me. And as time passed, I fell to the bottom of her list of priorities." Natasha's voice grew quieter. "And being a principal dancer changed her. It soon became clear that she wasn't the same girl I'd grown up with. She became bitter, petty, jealous, and obsessed with fame. It just got worse as she got older. Her career started to go south, which was inevitable. You know how it is."

Zoe nodded. Ballet dancers had short careers. It was one of many harsh truths about ballet.

"She was under lots of pressure," Natasha said. "And when younger dancers joined the company, ones who were better than her, it got worse. She just unraveled, and so did our relationship. We fought constantly, and we even broke up a few times, but we always ended up back together. We were miserable for years. But I'd been with her for so long, and I'd given up so much, that I wanted things to work out between us. I felt as if I had to prove to myself and to everyone else that I'd made the right decision choosing her. Otherwise, I'd wasted ten years of my life. Otherwise, I'd given up everything for nothing.

"Not to mention that the two of us had become so dependent on each other that I'd forgotten what a life without her was like. But as time went on, I knew things were well and truly over between us. That my love for her had died. So I made the decision to leave her. It was difficult, but I had to do it. It's taken me so long to feel like I can finally move on."

Natasha let out a breath, tension dissipating from her. Zoe wondered if Natasha had ever told anyone that story in full.

"These details? They're not important. What's important is that I made an impulsive decision based on my feelings rather than my head. I was young and naive, and I gave up everything for someone else. And I've spent over a decade living with regret for everything that could have been."

Natasha reached up and cupped Zoe's cheek in her hand. "Zoe. You're so much like I was at your age. So headstrong and passionate. And that's such a good thing. You would never be the dancer you are if you didn't feel as deeply as you do. You wouldn't be the beautiful, radiant woman you are."

Zoe's pulse sped up. Natasha's hand was soft and warm against her face.

"But the decisions you make right now will define your entire future. I don't want you to make the same mistake I did." Natasha's voice quivered. "And I can't bear the thought of being the one who holds you back from this incredible life that I know you're supposed to have."

Zoe felt a numbness in her chest. Natasha was right. She knew it in her mind, but she didn't want to accept it.

"So promise me," Natasha said. "Promise me you'll call up Riverside Ballet and turn down their offer. Promise me you'll buy a plane ticket, and pack your bags, and fly to London, and go live that dream you've been reaching for your whole life."

Tears formed in the corners of Zoe's eyes, but she didn't let them fall. "I will. I promise."

"That will make me happier than you staying here ever could."

Zoe chewed her lip. There were still things she wanted to say to Natasha.

But if this was the end of everything between them, there was no point saying them.

19

NATASHA

Natasha arrived at the restaurant her parents had picked out, Zoe by her side. Too late, she realized she hadn't told them that Zoe was coming. An awkward introduction was inevitable.

She looked around as they waited to be seated. Her eyes landed on a couple sitting by the window. Her parents.

It had been twenty years since Natasha last saw them, but they looked almost the same. Her mother had cut her hair short, and there was a splash of gray at her roots, but she had that same string of pearls around her neck that she wore everywhere. Her father was thinner than he used to be, and his hair was styled in a comb-over that failed to hide his bald spot.

They looked just like any other retired couple, although judging by their clothing, they were still more well-off than most. Although her family wasn't outrageously wealthy, Natasha had never wanted for anything as a child. Money, opportunity, love and support. But that all changed once her parents had found out about Paige.

Zoe squeezed her hand. "Are you ready?"

Natasha nodded and led Zoe over to her parents' table. The smile her mother gave her was strained. Her father looked at them, but his blank, hard expression didn't change. That was a side of herself Natasha had inherited from him.

She sat down, not bothering with a greeting. Zoe followed her lead.

"Natasha." Her mother's eyes flicked over to Zoe. "Who's this?"

"Mom, Dad, this is Zoe." Calling them Mom and Dad felt strange. "Zoe, this is Dina and Greg."

"Are the two of you..." Her mother looked Zoe up and down.

"Are you trying to ask if she's my girlfriend?"

"I suppose I am."

It was Zoe who replied. "Yes." She put her hand on Natasha's knee under the table. "I'm Natasha's girlfriend."

Natasha couldn't have chosen better backup. And although it was childish, it was satisfying to make her parents uncomfortable.

Dina plastered on a smile. "It's lovely to meet you, Zoe."

That was her mother all over. Her words were always polite, for the sake of being 'proper,' but the real meaning of her words was hidden in her tone. Natasha looked at her father. He'd always been the silent type, but so far, he hadn't said a word. Natasha wasn't complaining. As soon as he opened his mouth, the conversation would probably go downhill. Unlike her mother, he didn't care about hiding behind politeness.

A waiter came over to take their orders. Mercifully, her

parents only ordered main dishes, so Natasha and Zoe did the same. She didn't want to have to sit through multiple courses if everything went south.

The waiter left their table. Silence hung in the air. Natasha glanced at Zoe. She seemed completely unfazed by the palpable cloud of tension that loomed over them.

There's no point drawing this out. "What is it you want to tell me?" Natasha said.

"Now, let's not get ahead of ourselves," her mother replied. "Why don't we catch up first?"

"Catch up?" Natasha crossed her arms. "After all this time, you think we're just going to sit here and 'catch up?'"

"No need to take that tone, Natasha."

"What, so I'm supposed to just forget about everything that happened twenty years ago? And the fact that we haven't spoken at all since then?"

"I was hoping we could put all that"—Natasha's mother searched for a word—"unpleasantness behind us."

"*Unpleasantness?* Is that what you call cutting your eighteen-year-old daughter out of your lives?"

Her mother's hand flew to her chest as if Natasha's words had pierced her heart. "Cutting you out? We gave you a choice. You didn't have to run off with that girl. Do you have any idea how much that hurt your father and me?"

Natasha scoffed. "Do you actually think you were the victim in all this?"

"Do you think it was easy for us? What you did was a slap in the face to everything we've done for you."

"What I did? Or what I am?"

"It wasn't about the fact that you're a *lesbian*." Her mother could barely even say the word.

"Really? Because you made it clear that you didn't approve of my sexuality. Both of you did. You were always concerned about what was 'proper.' About what people would think."

"That's not true, Natasha," her mother said.

"Isn't it? Then if it was a boy I'd wanted to move away for? Would you have cut me off then?"

"Yes!"

Natasha gave her a sharp look, one she'd honed in her years teaching.

"Fine. Maybe we wouldn't have been quite as harsh as we were. But things were different back then. People like that, they didn't have easy lives."

"You mean gay people?

"Yes. We didn't want you to choose such a difficult path." Her mother held up her hands. "I know, it wasn't a choice. I realize that now. But, we just didn't want things to be hard for you."

"Like it was about me and my feelings. It was always about you and yours. If you cared about my feelings, you would have supported me, not tried to change me. All that pressure you put on me to be what you considered normal. All that effort you went to just to keep me from Paige and anything else you thought would influence me somehow. You were the ones who made life hard for me."

A pained expression crossed her mother's face, but this time, it seemed genuine. "We just wanted what was best for our only child. We made sure you had every opportunity, and that your future was bright. We made that ultimatum because we didn't want you to waste your life."

"You know what?" Natasha said. "All this time, I've

wondered if I wasted my life too. If I made the wrong choice by turning my back on my family and my future. Yes, it was foolish, running off for some girl. But it turns out, I wasn't throwing my life away. I was throwing away the life you wanted me to have. I would have never been happy if I'd chosen that life. I would have never been free to be myself because you never would have accepted me for who I am." Natasha stood up. "And if you still can't see that, then coming here was a mistake."

"Natasha, just try to understand—"

"No. I'm done." Natasha picked up her purse and slung it over her shoulder, then grabbed Zoe's hand "Let's go."

Her father cleared his throat. "I'm sorry."

Natasha turned to look at her father. These were the only words he'd spoken since she'd arrived. "Dad?"

"I'm sorry," he repeated. "We're both sorry. For cutting you out, for never accepting you for who you are. And Dina, we agreed that we wouldn't do this. Try to justify what we did."

Natasha looked at her mother. She wore a guilty grimace on her face.

"He's right," she said. "I'm sorry too, Natasha. We were wrong."

Natasha stood there, dumbfounded. She'd resigned herself to never hearing these words from her parents, but the day had finally come. She should have been elated. And a part of her was. But there was a question niggling in the back of her mind that wouldn't allow her to feel that happiness.

"Why?" she asked. "Why now?"

"Because we realized it was important that we reconcile," her mother said. "Before it's too late."

"Before what's too late?" Natasha looked from her mother to her father. His expression gave nothing away. "What's going on?"

"It's your father," her mother said. "The reason we're in the city is to see a specialist. An oncologist."

"An oncologist?" Natasha's stomach turned to ice. Somehow, she ended up back in her chair again. "But, that means cancer."

"Yes," her mother replied.

"No. Are you sure?" Natasha searched her father's face. Immediately, she knew that what her mother was saying was true. His thinness was unnatural, and his skin looked faded.

"We're sure," her mother said. "He was diagnosed a few years ago."

"Years?" Natasha's voice rose. "And you're just telling me now?"

"Well, the doctors thought it was treatable. And it was, at first. It went into remission quickly after initial treatments. But late last year, it came back, more aggressively this time. And it had spread, and there were no more treatment options."

"No more options," Natasha repeated.

"Well, no more options in terms of conventional treatments. The specialist here is a leader in his field. He's involved in some experimental new therapies that haven't been approved yet, but we're trying to get him into a trial."

Natasha's mother's voice faded into the background. Just moments ago, Natasha had been so furious with both of them. She'd been sure she'd never wanted to see them again. She'd thought that the side of her that still loved her parents had died. But it was still there. And she was still furious with them, but her anger was mixed with so many other emotions that she couldn't even identify.

"Natasha?"

She felt a hand on hers beneath the table. It was Zoe's. Natasha squeezed her hand back. Her mother had finished talking, although Natasha hadn't heard half of it.

"What are the chances of these experimental treatments working?" she asked.

It was her father who answered. "They're not good. If they do work, it'll give me a year or two more. But either way, it's terminal."

Natasha felt a sinking in her chest.

"It's why we wanted to reconnect. And to say we're sorry. We'd like to get to know you again." He turned to his wife. "Isn't that right?"

Natasha's mother nodded. "Yes. We'd both like it if we could just forget about the past and start fresh."

"I'm sorry. I'll never be able to forget the past." Natasha said. "But I am willing to start fresh."

"That's good enough for me," her mother said.

Silence fell over the table again, but this time, it wasn't tense. It was like they'd all been holding their breath, and now they could finally breathe again.

Her father cleared his throat. "So. You're teaching ballet now."

"Yes." Natasha almost laughed at the fact that they were making small talk after everything that had happened. It was going to take a while for them to become truly comfortable with each other.

Their food arrived. As the meal went on, so did the conversation. And bit by bit, they filled each other in on their respective lives. Her parents tried their best to get to know Zoe too. A few times, Natasha found herself laughing with them. But it was all weighed down by the knowledge that her newfound relationship with her father had a short expiration date.

As they finished with dinner, Natasha's mother sat back and sighed. "It sounds like you've made quite the life for yourself here. Are you happy?"

Natasha hesitated. If her mother had asked her the same question just weeks ago, Natasha wouldn't have known how to answer her. She'd felt stuck in place, trapped in a life that held little meaning, paralyzed by regrets and the choices she'd made. But now, none of that mattered.

Because, in a roundabout way, all those choices had led her to the woman sitting right next to her.

"Yes." Natasha looked at Zoe. "I am."

"Good for you. And I'm glad you've found someone." Her mother smiled at Zoe for the first time that night. "Look after her."

Zoe nodded. "I will."

They chatted for a few more minutes, then left the restaurant and went their separate ways with a promise to keep in touch. As soon as her parents were out of sight, Natasha was overcome by this wave of emotion that almost made her legs fall out from under her. Somehow, she managed to keep it contained.

"Are you all right?" Zoe asked.

No, she wanted to say. But if she opened her mouth to say what she really felt, she wouldn't be able to stop herself from falling apart. Instead, she asked a simple question. "Come home with me?"

Natasha wasn't sure exactly what she wanted from Zoe. She just knew she wanted Zoe there.

"Sure," Zoe replied.

20

NATASHA

When they arrived back at her apartment, Natasha tossed her keys onto the table and headed into the kitchen. She poured herself a glass of water. She wasn't even thirsty. She just needed something to do to distract herself.

"Natasha?" Zoe said. "How are you doing?"

She put the glass down. "I don't know. I don't know how I'm doing. I don't know how to feel."

Zoe took Natasha's hand and wrapped her fingers around it.

"It's strange," Natasha said. "After my parents apologized, I was happy. For a moment, I forgot all about everything that had happened between us. For a moment, I had a family again." She struggled to keep her voice from shaking. "But now my father is going to be taken away from me. And I don't feel sad. I just feel angry. Why didn't my parents do this sooner? It took one of them almost dying to reach out to me! And why did they even bother? Why did they give me hope when it can't last?"

"You still have time," Zoe said. "You can still have a relationship with them again."

"But what's the point? What's the point of any of this if my father is just going to die on me? And my mother, she's getting older. She's not going to live forever." Natasha's hand curled into a fist. "I wish I hadn't gone to dinner with them. I wish they hadn't contacted me in the first place. I wish everything was just like it was before."

"Oh, Natasha. I'm sorry." Zoe stretched out her arms and pulled Natasha into her. "It'll be okay."

Only then did Natasha realize she was trembling. She closed her eyes and wrapped her arms around Zoe in return until all those emotions boiling inside her reduced to a dull ache deep in her chest.

Natasha broke away. "I sound crazy. It's just, all this is so unexpected. Seeing my parents. Their apology. Being confronted with the fact that they're not going to be around forever." She sighed. "I guess all I can do is try to make use of the time I have with them."

"Yeah," Zoe said. "It's something, at least."

Natasha smiled weakly. "Thanks for coming along. I thought I was going to need backup, but I needed support more. I don't know what I would have done without you."

"Any time."

"I think my mother actually likes you. That's a first. My parents, meeting my girlfriend. I never thought that would happen."

"Er, about that," Zoe said. "Girlfriend seemed like the right thing to say at the time. I hope you don't mind."

"I did introduce you to my parents. And you won them over. That makes you my girlfriend."

Zoe smiled. Natasha leaned over and kissed her. As soon as their lips touched, Natasha was flooded with an insatiable sense of urgency. She parted Zoe's lips with her own, kissing her harder. Zoe exhaled sharply and stepped in closer, her body rippling against Natasha's.

Natasha pushed Zoe back against the countertop and wrapped her fingers around Zoe's wrists. A murmur fell from Zoe's lips, her hooded gaze filled with desire.

"I want you so much right now," Natasha said softly.

Natasha smothered Zoe's lips with her own, their tongues twirling around each other. She brought a hand to the back of Zoe's head, and let the other roam down her sides, grabbing wildly at her slight curves.

Zoe groped at Natasha's body in return. Her ferocity only doubled Natasha's. No matter how hungry Zoe's hands were, Natasha's were hungrier. No matter how hard Zoe kissed her, Natasha kissed her harder. And every whimper that fell from Zoe's lips only invigorated her.

Their lips still locked, Natasha dragged the hem of Zoe's dress up her thigh and guided her hand between Zoe's legs. Her panties were wet already.

"Natasha." Zoe's voice dripped with need.

Natasha pressed a finger to the other woman's lips in a silent command. She didn't need Zoe's words to know what she wanted. She reached under Zoe's dress, searching for the waistband of her panties, and pulled them down Zoe's narrow hips.

"Get onto the counter," she said.

Zoe hoisted herself up. Natasha yanked Zoe's underwear from her legs and flung them aside, then shoved Zoe's shoulders down onto the countertop. Something fell to the floor with a metallic clatter. The fruit bowl? Natasha didn't care. All she cared about was ravishing the irresistible woman who was lying half-naked on her counter with her legs clenched around Natasha's waist.

Natasha leaned down and kissed her greedily, pushing Zoe's dress up. She slid her hands up underneath it to caress Zoe's breasts. Her nipples tightened at Natasha's touch. Zoe ground back against her, setting off a fire inside Natasha's core. She grazed her hands down Zoe's sides, letting her fingertips dig into Zoe's supple, bronze skin. Gasping, Zoe ground into Natasha even harder.

She grabbed hold of Zoe's ass cheeks and kissed her way down Zoe's smooth, toned stomach. Lying back with her dress spread around her, Zoe looked like a divine being from a work of art.

Natasha pushed Zoe's knees even further apart and ran her hands up her inner thighs. Natasha followed the trail of fingertips with her lips, higher and higher until she could feel the searing heat where Zoe's legs met, tempting her to bury herself between them. Instead, Natasha continued to tease her, relishing the way Zoe's body reacted to the slightest of her touches. The shivers, the moans—they drove Natasha wild.

It was all too much for her. Natasha swept her mouth up to the peak of Zoe's thighs and pushed her tongue between her lips. It was liquid silk, all smooth, slick and warm. And Zoe's scent was heavenly.

Above her, Zoe let out a groan. "God, yes."

Natasha barely heard her. She was too busy getting lost between Zoe's thighs. Her tongue swirled and her lips sucked, raining pleasure all over Zoe's pussy. Her outer lips, which were covered in the finest, softest coat of hair. Her satiny inner lips. Her entrance, which seemed to pulse when Natasha darted her tongue inside.

When she reached the little hidden pearl at the apex of Zoe's slit, she wrapped her lips around it and sucked gently. A tremble rolled through Zoe's body. Her mouth still working between Zoe's legs, Natasha peered up at her. She was propped up on her forearms, hands splayed on the marble countertop, her face contorted with bliss.

"Please," Zoe murmured.

Natasha dug her fingers into Zoe's ass cheeks and redoubled her efforts, devouring her. Zoe squirmed and bucked greedily.

Seconds later, her hips rose into Natasha's face and her body stiffened. A wild cry flew from Zoe's lips and echoed through the kitchen.

Zoe blew out a hard breath. After a moment, she raised herself up to sit upright and drew Natasha to her, kissing her greedily. Natasha broke off, only to whisper into Zoe's ear.

"I want you to fuck me."

Natasha turned them both around so that her back was against the counter. Her eyes locked on Zoe's, she reached under her pencil skirt and slid her panties down from under it. Instantly, Natasha could sense the heat flaring up in Zoe once more.

Natasha yanked her close, kissing her again. Zoe's hands glided down between them to tug Natasha's blouse out of her skirt. She fumbled with the buttons, slowly exposing Natasha's bra-covered breasts. After getting a few buttons open, Zoe gave up, instead opting to pull the cups of

Natasha's bra down, baring her breasts. Zoe kneaded them with her fingertips, then drew her mouth down to kiss them all over.

Natasha moaned softly. Zoe flicked the tip of her tongue against one of Natasha's nipples and swirled it around them, then sucked on them firmly, one after the other.

"Zoe," Natasha said. "Fuck me. Fuck me now."

Her mouth still working at Natasha's breasts, Zoe slid her hands down to tug Natasha's skirt up past her hips. The air felt cool against Natasha's bare legs. Zoe slipped her finger into Natasha's slit, sending a tremor through her.

Zoe lingered at her clit for a moment, eliciting a desperate hiss from Natasha. She ran her finger down, seeking Natasha's entrance, and dipped it inside. Another finger followed.

Natasha pushed out toward her.

Slowly, Zoe plunged deeper. Natasha shuddered and leaned back against the countertop, satisfaction suffusing every part of her body. Zoe thrust back and forth, her fingers curling inside in the most delicious way. Her thumb reached up to roll over Natasha's nub.

"Don't stop." Natasha was already so close. She'd been aching for Zoe from the moment she'd kissed her.

Zoe delved deeper, reaching depths inside Natasha that no one ever had before. Her fingers curled around the edge of the hard marble counter, gripping so hard that her fingertips grew numb. Zoe leaned in and painted kisses down the side of her neck.

"Oh yes!" An eruption went off deep in Natasha's body, tearing through her unrelentingly. She arched toward Zoe, pressing hard into her, drawing out even more pleasure.

When she slumped back onto the counter on her elbows, Zoe dipped to kiss her, long and slow.

Natasha stared up at the ceiling. Somehow, they'd ended up in her bed, where they'd continued their frantic lovemaking until both of them were too worn out to move. And now that it was over, that weight in Natasha's chest had returned.

Natasha peered at Zoe. She was lying back against the pillows, a satisfied grin on her face.

"Whew," Zoe said. "I don't think I can ever get out of this bed."

Natasha felt a pang of unease. The way she'd pounced on Zoe, when minutes before she'd been struggling to keep herself together. Had she used Zoe to make herself feel better? Why else had Natasha wanted her so badly at that moment?

"Hey." Zoe drew a zig-zagging line up Natasha's arm. "What's going on in that head of yours?"

"I'm just wondering if it's messed up that we just did what we did right after I found out my father is dying," Natasha said.

"I don't think it's messed up." Zoe rolled onto her side to face Natasha. "Sex can be comforting. Not to mention life-affirming. And after this evening, I can see why you'd feel the urge to do something life-affirming."

Natasha hoped that was all it was. She didn't like the idea of screwing Zoe around. Zoe was far too important to her to make that mistake again.

Natasha brushed back one of Zoe's curls. "When did you become so wise?"

"It's been ten years," Zoe said. "Do you really think I'm the same idealistic teenager I was back then?"

"I guess not." The gap between the two of them had shrunk. Zoe had grown and changed. Had Natasha changed at all?

Zoe snuggled in closer, draping her arm across Natasha's stomach. They lay in silence for a while, eyes closed, breathing each other in. That hollow feeling in Natasha's chest began to dissipate.

"Natasha?" Zoe looked up at her.

"Yes?" Natasha murmured.

"Do you remember that night? The night before I left for London. When I came to your house."

"Yes." How could Natasha forget it?

"I came here to tell you I loved you."

Natasha knew. She'd always known. Which was why it had pained her to break Zoe's heart the way she did.

"You were my first love. These past ten years, nothing has compared to what I felt for you back then. No one else has compared to you. I know you wanted me too, but I never could forget you."

"I never forgot you either," Natasha said. "And I'm sorry. About that night. About... about the way I handled things."

"You don't have to apologize," Zoe said. "It took me a while, but I understand why you did what you did. Love, relationships. They're complicated. You and Paige had a long history."

It was true. Natasha's relationship with Paige had been complicated. But that was the only thing Zoe had gotten right. There was far more between Natasha and Paige than Zoe understood. Far more to that night than Zoe knew. But right now, after the day she'd just had, Natasha didn't want to revisit that hellish night.

"Whatever happened between you and Paige?" Zoe asked. "You know, after I moved away?"

Natasha hesitated. "It didn't work out."

Mercifully, Zoe didn't pry. She just rested her head on Natasha's shoulder and closed her eyes again.

However, one thing was certain. Eventually, she would have to tell Zoe everything.

21

ZOE

*I*t had been the night before Zoe was due to leave for London.

She'd been lying on her bed, staring vacantly at a faded ballet poster that hung on the wall beside her. Her bedroom had looked so empty with everything packed away. Her suitcase was on the floor at the foot of the bed. Her plane ticket and passport were sitting on her desk. Her alarm was set for 5 a.m. so she wouldn't miss her early morning flight.

She'd kept her promise to Natasha and had taken the position with the Royal London Ballet immediately. Natasha was right. She couldn't give up her dreams for someone else. At least, that was what her mind told her.

But her heart? It said something entirely different.

Zoe sighed. Normally, she'd be wrapping up a class with Natasha right now. She was going to miss those lessons. And she was going to miss Natasha. The thought of never seeing her again made Zoe ache down to her bones.

Zoe sat up. She had to do something. She knew the two

of them couldn't possibly be together. But she had to tell Natasha how she felt—how she *really* felt—before it was too late.

She grabbed her phone from the nightstand. Natasha had given Zoe her number for emergencies. This counted as an emergency. She typed out a message to Natasha. *Can I come see you? I want to talk.*

She pressed send and fell back down onto her bed. A minute passed, then five, then ten. Nothing. Zoe didn't have time to wait around. She was going to be on a plane to London in less than twelve hours. She had to see Natasha before it was too late.

Silencing the voice in her head that was telling her how crazy this was, Zoe got up, grabbed the keys to the car she shared with her sister and headed outside. She knew where Natasha lived. They'd stopped by her house once, after Zoe had won the World Grand Prix. Although Zoe hadn't been inside, she remembered the address. It was only a few streets away from the academy.

By the time Zoe reached Natasha's house, her heart was racing. It was getting late. Too late to show up on someone's doorstep unannounced. Zoe didn't care now. Natasha would still be awake.

As she reached Natasha's door, she felt a sudden surge of anxiety. Was this a bad idea? Everything between the two of them had had always felt so tenuous. Although Zoe was certain of her feelings for Natasha, Natasha had always pushed her away when she got too close. She knew Natasha felt something for her. But there was a big difference between 'something,' and what Zoe felt for Natasha.

Zoe steeled herself and knocked.

Moments later, Natasha opened the door. "Zoe? What are you doing here?"

"I came to see you," Zoe said. "I want to talk to you."

"I can't talk right now."

There was a hint of conflict in Natasha's face. But Zoe pressed on. "Please, Natasha. There's something I need to tell you."

Natasha glanced over her shoulder and stepped outside, shutting the door behind her. "What's this about?"

"I'm leaving tomorrow. But I still don't want to leave you."

"We've talked about this. You have to live your life for yourself, not anyone else."

"I know. And I've accepted that. But I need you to know that you're not just anyone else." Zoe took a deep breath. "I've never felt this way about anyone before. We have this incredible connection which I can't ignore."

"Now isn't the time, Zoe."

"It's the only time. I have to tell you how I feel before it's too late—"

"Zoe, stop." Natasha held up her hands, palms out. "What I mean is, we can't do this now. I'm not alone."

Zoe frowned. "What do you mean?"

The door swung open. Standing in the doorway was a woman Zoe had never met. But Zoe knew her face. Every ballet dancer in the country knew her face and that trademark blonde hair. Everyone knew her name.

Paige Collins.

Zoe's stomach dropped.

"Nat?" Paige's eyes fell on Zoe. Her lip curled with disdain. "Who's this?"

"Just one of my students," Natasha said. "Something important came up."

Paige scoured Zoe with her eyes once more, then draped a hand on Natasha's shoulder. "Don't take too long."

"I won't."

Paige went back inside, leaving the door open behind her, and sat down on the couch. Zoe could still see her from where she stood.

"Natasha?" Zoe kept her voice low. "What's Paige doing here?" She already knew the answer. There was only one reason Paige would be at Natasha's house late at night. It was made even clearer by the affectionate touch Paige gave her, and the way Natasha had referred to Zoe as 'just a student.' "Are the two of you back together?"

"It's complicated," Natasha said softly. "Things between us have always been. But I can't talk about this now."

"But I thought..." Clearly, Zoe hadn't thought at all. At once, the pieces began to fall into place. Zoe had always felt like Paige had this mysterious grip on Natasha. Zoe knew there had to be some deeper reason why. But apparently, the reason was simple. Natasha's heart still belonged to her.

Zoe hadn't stood a chance.

"I should go," Natasha said. "Zoe, I'm sorry."

"It's okay," Zoe said. "I understand. You were right about everything. About us." Zoe should never have come here. She should have let things be.

Natasha lingered in the doorway, her whole body taut. She lifted her hand, as if to reach for Zoe one last time.

Instead, her arm fell back down to her side. She gave Zoe a weak smile. "Goodbye, Zoe," she whispered. "And good luck."

It wasn't until Natasha shut the door that Zoe let the tears she'd been holding back fall.

22
ZOE

Zoe took a seat at a table in the corner of the restaurant. She was a few minutes late, but Gillian, her former colleague and friend, hadn't arrived yet.

She sat back and waited. Over the past few days, she'd started taking steps toward finding a job in the city. She'd heard through the grapevine that Gillian, a former choreographer for the Royal London Ballet who Zoe knew well, was starting her own small ballet company right here in the city. Zoe had gotten in touch, and she and Gillian had made plans to catch up over lunch to discuss Zoe joining her venture. Gillian's business partner was coming to lunch too, but Zoe hadn't met her.

"Zoe Waters. It's been too long."

Zoe looked up to see a short, middle-aged woman with dark, shoulder-length hair. It had been years since Gillian left the Royal London Ballet, and they hadn't seen each other since then, but Gillian looked exactly the same, save for the streaks of gray in her hair.

Zoe stood up and embraced her warmly. "It's so good to see you."

"My partner in crime is on her way." Gillian sat down across from Zoe. "She'll be here any minute. She told me what to order for her, so we won't have to wait. And it'll give us a chance to catch up."

They made small talk while Zoe browsed the menu. Soon, the topic of Zoe's injury came up.

"I heard about what happened," Gillian said. "How are you holding up?"

"It's taken a lot of adjusting, but I'm doing okay," Zoe replied.

Gillian gave her a sympathetic smile. "I've been there. The same thing happened to me."

"Really?" Zoe knew Gillian had been a dancer decades ago, but she didn't know much about her career.

"It was opening night. I was dancing a pas de deux. My oaf of a partner dropped me on stage. I snapped a tendon in my knee."

Zoe winced. "Ouch."

"The fact that it ruined the show hurt far more than my knee. But it wasn't so bad in the end. It gave me an excuse to quit dancing and pursue things behind the scenes. Choreography, and now directing, if we can get this company off the ground." Gillian clasped her hands on the table in front of her. "But let's not jump into business so quickly. I want to hear about what you've been up to these past few years."

Zoe filled Gillian in on her life since they'd last seen each other. By the time the waitress came over to take their orders, the conversation had moved on to old colleagues and friends, who had scattered all over the world.

This part of the conversation was more one-sided. Unlike Zoe, Gillian had kept in touch with everyone. She had all the gossip. And she liked to talk.

Twenty minutes later, Gillian was telling Zoe about her recent divorce in great detail, and Zoe was beginning to wonder if she should try to steer her toward the topic of her new dance company. Before Zoe got the chance, they were interrupted by a slender blonde woman.

"Sorry I'm late," the woman said.

Zoe looked at her face and froze. She knew that face. She had only seen it in person once, but it had been etched in her memory ever since.

"Paige, you're here." Gillian gestured toward Zoe. "Paige, this is Zoe Waters. Zoe, this is Paige Collins, my business partner."

Zoe gaped at her. Paige was the last person she was expecting to run into. The look on Paige's face suggested that she felt the same way. Did Paige know who Zoe was?

Gillian looked from Paige to Zoe. "Do the two of you know each other?"

"We've met," Paige said coldly.

Well, that settled it. Paige obviously wasn't thrilled about Zoe's presence, but Zoe didn't know why exactly. Had Natasha told Paige about her at some point after they'd gotten back together?

Right on cue, their food arrived. *Great. Now I have to sit through lunch with Natasha's ex-girlfriend.* Zoe didn't hate Paige. But seeing her brought up all the memories and feelings of that fateful night. Zoe hadn't blamed Natasha for what happened. Sure, she'd been heartbroken at first. But she'd never held it against Natasha. She'd never seen it as Natasha rejecting her.

At least, that was what Zoe told herself. But with Paige sitting right in front of her, she couldn't help but feel the sting to that rejection. It didn't help that Paige kept giving her dirty looks. Zoe might have been imagining it. Paige Collins had always had a reputation for being cold and snobby.

Gillian was oblivious to it all. "I was just telling Zoe about that date I went on. The one with that man who started crying about his ex-wife halfway through dinner. I swear dating never used to be this awful when I was in my twenties." She turned to Zoe, a spark in her eye. "But that's enough about me. Zoe, is there a special someone in your life?"

"Uh, yes." Zoe glanced at Paige. She wasn't sure how to explain her relationship with Natasha at the best of times, let alone with Natasha's ex sitting right there.

But she didn't have to elaborate. Gillian did that for her. "So it's true then? You and an old teacher of yours? One of the instructors at the National Academy?"

Zoe cursed internally. News traveled fast in the dance community. "Yes, it's true." She avoided Paige's gaze, but she could feel it on her.

"Really?" Gillian examined Zoe with a knowing smile. "Apparently you've been flitting about town going to shows together. And you got caught by students canoodling in one of the academy's studios."

Zoe sighed. "That's not what happened."

Paige set her glass down on the table with a loud thud. "Shouldn't we be talking about our company?"

"Of course," Gillian said. "Sorry, we got carried away. You know how it is, catching up with old friends."

Gillian began telling Zoe about their plans for the new ballet company. It would be small, local, and would focus on a more contemporary style. But with Paige's eyes on her, Zoe was finding it difficult to concentrate on Gillian's words. Paige was making no effort to hide her disdain for Zoe.

Midway through lunch, Gillian's phone rang.

"I should take this. I'll be right back." Gillian got up, and scurried out of the restaurant, leaving Zoe and Paige alone at the table.

Zoe glanced at Paige. Should she try to make small talk? Ask Paige about the company? Sit there in uncomfortable silence?

Paige folded her arms on her chest and looked Zoe up and down. "Zoe Waters," she said. "So, the rumors of your retirement are true."

"I haven't made any firm decisions yet," Zoe replied.

"You're kidding yourself if you think you can make a comeback after this. How does it feel, knowing your days in the spotlight are over?"

"It was never about the spotlight for me."

"Sure it wasn't." Paige smirked. "Of course, everyone knows that the only reason you were in the spotlight in the first place was to fill the Royal London Ballet's diversity quota."

Zoe set down her knife and fork, fuming inside. "What's your problem?"

"Why don't you take a guess?" Paige said.

"This is about Natasha."

"Of course it is. I'm not one to hold grudges, but do you really expect me to play nice with the woman who came between me and the love of my life?"

"How could I possibly have come between you?" Zoe asked. "Natasha and I only just started seeing each other."

"Don't play dumb with me," Paige hissed. "I'm talking about back when you were her student."

How did Paige know about that? Had Natasha told her? It still didn't explain why Paige thought Zoe had come between them.

"I knew there was someone else," Paige said. "Some reason Natasha didn't want to mend our relationship. I just didn't know who it was until you showed up at her door. Natasha denied it, and I foolishly believed her. But it was obvious. A student showing up at her house late at night? You were that someone else. You're the one who stole her from me."

"I didn't steal Natasha from you," Zoe said. "Firstly, when Natasha and I met, the two of you were broken up. And secondly, nothing happened between us. Not really. That night made it abundantly clear that it was you she chose, not me."

"I don't know what you're talking about."

"Yes, you do. She went back to you."

Confusion crossed Paige's face. "No, she didn't."

Zoe frowned. "Natasha said the two of you got back together."

"Is that what she told you? Apparently, I wasn't the only one she lied to."

"What? But, you were at her house that night. I saw you."

"I was there to pick up some stuff I'd left at her place. We got talking, and I tried to fix things between us. To work things out. But Natasha refused, because of you. That was the last night I ever saw her."

Zoe shook her head. "This doesn't make sense. I don't believe you."

"I'm not that petty. You're the one who brought it up. I'm just telling you what happened."

Was Paige telling the truth? Then why had Natasha said otherwise? Zoe trusted Natasha more than Paige. But when she thought back to that night, something stood out to her. Although her memory was a little hazy, Natasha had never actually said that she and Paige were back together. It was Zoe who had come to that conclusion.

If it had been a simple misunderstanding, Natasha would have corrected her. But the alternative was much worse. The alternative was that Natasha had misled Zoe on purpose.

Zoe had to clear things up. "Tell Gillian I'll call her later." She stood up. "I have to go."

Zoe stormed into the academy. It was a Friday afternoon, so Natasha would be in her studio. Hopefully, Zoe could catch her between lessons. If she was busy, Zoe could wait. She had to know the truth.

She reached Natasha's studio. It was filled with students performing their pre-class stretches. Natasha weaved through them, speaking with each of them as she passed by. A few of the students spotted Zoe in the doorway. Whispers broke out between them.

It didn't take long for Natasha to notice her. She broke off from a cluster of students and walked over to the door. "What are you doing here? Is everything okay?"

"No," Zoe said. "It's not."

Natasha took Zoe's elbow and steered her down the hall, out of earshot of her students. "What's going on?"

"Remember that lunch I told you about? With that friend of mine and her business partner? It was today. And her business partner was Paige."

The color drained from Natasha's face. The same thing had happened when Zoe had mentioned Paige the other night. She hadn't known why at the time. But now she knew it was because of guilt.

"She told me something interesting," Zoe continued. "She said that the two of you never got back together."

Natasha glanced toward the studio. "We shouldn't be talking about this here."

"I don't care." Zoe crossed her arms. "Is it true?"

Natasha's mouth opened then closed again.

"Natasha. Tell me Paige is lying. Tell me she's just a jealous ex trying to cause trouble."

For a moment, Natasha was silent.

"I can't," Natasha said. "It's true."

Zoe felt a wrenching in her chest. "Why? All this time, I thought you went back to her. And don't tell me it was some misunderstanding. You knew I believed the two of you were back together. And you let me keep believing that for ten whole years. If you didn't want me to think that, you would have said something."

"You're right," Natasha said. "I'm sorry."

"Why, Natasha?"

"I had no choice."

"What does that even mean?" Zoe thought back to that night, and everything leading up to it. About how Natasha had told Zoe not to stay in the city for her. "Let me guess. You were trying to get rid of me? To push me away 'for my own good?'" She scoffed. "That's so typical of you."

"That's not what it was about. Not really. I mean, it's why I kept the truth from you, but- it's complicated."

"You always say that. *It's complicated.*" Zoe threw her hands up. "It looks pretty simple from where I'm standing. You said so yourself, that you didn't want me to throw away my life for you. That you wanted me to forget you. Is that why you did it? To crush any ideas I had about the two of us ever being together?"

Natasha didn't answer.

Zoe shook her head. "That night, I went to your house to tell you I loved you, and you shut me down. You made me think that your heart belonged to someone else." She swallowed the lump that had formed in her throat. "But I told myself it wasn't about me. I told myself that I couldn't compete with all that history you and Paige had." Zoe's clenched her fists. "But it turns out, that was never the case. You were just lying to me all along."

"Zoe, please," Natasha said. "Let's just talk about this."

"I don't want to talk about this," she yelled. "You always saw me as this child with a crush. You never took my feelings seriously, or you never would have lied to get rid of me. You said yourself that everything between us was just because you were lonely. And that hasn't changed, or else you wouldn't have kept this from me for ten whole years!"

Natasha reached for Zoe's arm. "Zoe-"

"No." Zoe looked down the hall and into Natasha's studio. A few of her students were standing within full view of the door, pretending not to watch the scene that was unfolding. "Your class is waiting for you."

Natasha glanced toward the studio, a torn expression on her face. "Zoe, please."

"Just go. Teach your class." Zoe turned and fled down the hall.

23

NATASHA

Natasha watched her students leap across the room in groups, offering advice and words of encouragement now and then. The class was almost over. Natasha was trying her hardest to remain focused, but her mind kept on drifting back to Zoe.

It had been a few days since their fight, and Natasha hadn't spoken to her since. She'd been debating whether to reach out, to apologize and to explain herself. But every time she thought about it, she remembered the pain of betrayal on Zoe's face, and the tears that Zoe had tried to hide, and she felt a guilty gnawing in her stomach.

She'd done what she'd feared doing all along. She'd crushed Zoe's heart again.

Natasha watched the next group perform the exercise. Megan, the student of hers who had been so star-struck by Zoe, was among them. As usual, her technique was flawless. Although Megan wasn't one of her private students, she was a favorite of Natasha's. She had a bright future ahead of her.

When she was done, Natasha yelled some praise in her direction, patting her on the back as she passed. Megan beamed. She was so like Zoe, so talented and full of life. When she danced, she had that same spark, and that star quality. No wonder she and Zoe had gotten along so well.

Natasha sighed. She missed that spark of Zoe's. Would Zoe ever forgive her, even if she did explain herself? Or was it too late? If she'd just told Zoe the truth earlier on, or even when Zoe had confronted her days ago, they wouldn't be in this mess. But that wound had been too painful for Natasha to open when put on the spot like that. She'd been paralyzed, unable to do or say anything other than utter feeble apologies.

No, she was just making excuses for her unforgivable behavior. Maybe she should just accept that things between herself and Zoe could never be, just like she should have ten years ago.

"Okay everyone," Natasha said. "That's all for the day."

The students curtsied and bowed to Natasha, then began to pack up and leave. Megan, however, made a beeline for her teacher.

"Natasha?" Megan said.

Natasha blinked, clearing her head. "What can I do for you?"

"I want to talk about my audition on the weekend. I've been struggling with my fouettes in class, and I'm worried that it's going to hurt my chances."

Megan blurted out a long list of concerns, her voice wavering. It was clear that she needed a pep talk more than anything. Natasha had gotten better at those over time. If teaching Zoe all those years ago had taught her one thing, it was that there was a time to be firm, and a time to show a softer side.

"Megan," Natasha said. "Stop worrying about all the things that could go wrong. You're one of the most hard-working students in your class. You have passion and enthusiasm in spades. And you dance so beautifully. Have faith in yourself. You can do this."

"You're right." Megan nodded to herself. "I can do this."

"You're going to do wonderfully."

"Thanks." Megan hesitated before her.

"Is there something else?"

"I was wondering. Is Zoe coming back to teach us again? I really liked that lesson with her. It was fun."

'Fun' was one way to describe it. Natasha would have used the word 'chaotic.' But the students had loved it. Zoe seemed to have that effect on everyone. There was this magic about her that lit every room she was in, this heartfelt passion that made everyone around her feel so alive. Natasha felt a twinge of sadness deep in her chest at the thought that she'd hurt Zoe so badly.

"I don't think Zoe's coming back," she said.

"Oh," Megan said. "That's too bad. I hope everything is okay with the two of you."

Even the students knew about Zoe and Natasha? Their loud, public fight just outside the studio probably didn't help. "Don't you worry about that," Natasha said. "Is there anything else you'd like to talk about before your audition?"

"No, I'm good. Thanks." Megan said goodbye and left the room.

Natasha looked around the empty studio. For the last ten years, whenever she was alone in the studio, she would take a moment to close her eyes and remember the lessons she'd had in here with Zoe. Those lessons had made Natasha's teaching job feel worth it.

And ever since she came crashing back into Natasha's world, she'd made Natasha's whole life feel worth it.

Natasha steeled herself. She could either stay here, feeling sorry for herself, or she could apologize to Zoe and try to work things out between them.

She packed up the studio and headed to Zoe's apartment.

Natasha knocked on Zoe's door. While she waited, she prayed that Zoe would hear her out. But she wouldn't be surprised if Zoe simply slammed the door in her face. She probably deserved it.

The door opened, but the woman who answered wasn't Zoe. She was like a taller, wider version of Zoe, with a more serious face, and a much more imposing countenance.

"Can I help you?" the woman asked.

"You're Zoe's sister," Natasha said. They'd met once before. And this was her apartment, after all.

"Yep. I'm Dawn. If you're looking for Zoe, you just missed her."

"Do you know when she'll be back?"

"Not any time soon," Dawn said. "She's gone back to London."

Natasha's heart dropped. "What? When?"

"No idea. I've been off the grid for a while, so we haven't spoken much. When I came back last night, the place was empty. She left me a note. It said she was going back to London, and she'd talk to me soon. I knew she wasn't planning to stick around for too long, but I wasn't expecting her to leave so quickly."

"No, that can't be right." Natasha and Zoe had just begun planning a life together. "She wouldn't just leave like that."

But as the words left her mouth, she knew it was true. It was exactly what Zoe would do. Her heart had been crushed, so she wanted to get as far away from Natasha as possible. Even if that meant putting the entire world between them again.

Dawn frowned. "Is something going on with her that I should know about? Now that I think about it, she hasn't answered the text I sent her."

"No," Natasha said. "I'm sure she'll fill you in." If they were as close as Zoe said they were, it would be Dawn whose shoulder Zoe cried on.

Dawn folded her arms over her chest. "You seem familiar. Have we met before?"

"Once. It was a long time ago."

"I'm sorry. I don't remember. Who are you exactly?"

"I'm no one." *Just some idiot who screwed up everything.*

"Right." Dawn looked her up and down skeptically. "Should I tell Zoe you stopped by?"

"No, don't worry about it." It was easiest this way. Zoe deserved a clean break. "Thanks."

Dawn gave her a confused smile, then shut the door.

It was too late. Once again, Natasha and Zoe were at opposite sides of the world, heartbroken and alone. She'd gotten a second chance with Zoe, and she'd blown it. She'd lost Zoe again.

And now, she'd run out of chances.

24

ZOE

Zoe stared through the office window and out into the city beyond. She could distantly hear the director speaking to those gathered in the room. Everyone there was part of the Royal London Ballet's outreach team. As of a few hours ago, this included Zoe.

She'd arrived back in London only days ago, with no solid plan or goals. This morning, she went to see the director of the company to finally have that conversation about her future. He offered her a position on the Royal London Ballet's outreach program. Its purpose was to bring ballet to people who wouldn't otherwise have any exposure to it. Adults, who would hopefully become fans. Young kids, who might be inspired to take classes, just like Zoe had been all those years ago. It was all about keeping the art of ballet alive.

Zoe had said yes to the job immediately. It was perfect for her. She'd get to spread her passion for ballet and introduce people to a world that she loved. Plus, it was a mix of performing, demonstrating, and teaching. After that lesson with Natasha, she'd slowly come around to the idea of becoming a teacher.

She should have been thrilled. She was doing what she loved, and she was among friends again, people she'd forged strong relationships with over the last ten years. And she was home. She hadn't realized it until she'd left London, but this city felt like home more than anywhere else she'd lived. In moving here and joining the company, she'd found her community, a place where she belonged.

But right now, she just felt hollow and alone.

Everyone around her began to file out of the room. Zoe joined them. She hoped nothing important had been said during the meeting. She'd been lost in her head the entire time.

Her new boss, an older woman with a friendly smile, stopped her at the door. "I'm glad you're back with us, Zoe. I know this job isn't as exciting as being on stage, but I think you'll enjoy it."

"I'm happy to be here," Zoe said. "I can't wait to get started."

"Why don't you start by coming up with some lesson plans? Something we can use as a fun introduction to ballet."

"Sure. I can do that."

Zoe said goodbye to her boss and all her new coworkers. It was the end of the day, and everyone was leaving the office. Zoe left the building and headed home. It was only a few minutes away. She had snapped up the little terrace house years ago because it was close to the Royal London Ballet's headquarters where she'd trained and rehearsed every day.

It was evening, and the sun was already setting. Zoe hurried along, eager to get out of the cold. She thought about the task her boss had given her as she walked. She couldn't help but wonder what Natasha would have to say about her new job.

Something pulled in her chest. She missed Natasha so deeply. But at the same time, just the thought of her made Zoe feel sick with betrayal. Natasha had lied to her. Not just now, but for ten years. And for stupid, controlling reasons.

At least, that was what she thought. But when she replayed their fight in her head, it was obvious that Natasha had wanted to say more. Zoe hadn't given her a chance. She hadn't wanted to hear her excuses. But what if she'd been wrong? What if Natasha really did have a good reason for doing what she did?

What if Zoe had thrown everything away without knowing the whole truth?

It was so typical of her, to act without thinking. She didn't even remember making the decision to move back to London. After the fight with Natasha, she'd simply packed her bags and gotten on the next flight out. She'd tried to run from her feelings, just like she had when she'd left London in the first place.

It wasn't until she'd gotten off the plane that she realized what she'd done. Zoe had put thousands of miles between herself and the woman who had captured her heart and held onto it for ten whole years. She'd made it impossible for them to be together for a second time. And in doing so, she'd made it clear to Natasha that she never wanted to see her again. It didn't help that she'd gone to Natasha's workplace and made a scene. Natasha was probably furious at her. Not that Zoe cared.

She sighed. Maybe it was time to call her sister and talk about everything. Zoe had been avoiding Dawn's calls because she would immediately know from Zoe's voice that something was wrong. And then she'd have to explain how she'd lost the love of her life ten years ago, then they'd found each other again, only for them to mess everything up, for good this time.

As she neared her townhouse, Zoe noticed someone standing on her front step. A woman in a long black coat, with dark brown hair and even darker eyes. Her heart jumped.

Natasha.

Zoe slowed to a halt. From several feet away, Natasha's eyes fell on her. She gave Zoe a tight smile. Zoe's heart pounded even harder. Natasha was here. In London.

For her.

Relief washed over for her, but her anger and uncertainty quickly returned. Despite it all, she had this urge to run up to Natasha and throw her arms around her.

Instead, Zoe walked over to her slowly. "Natasha. What are you doing here?"

"I needed to see you. I need to talk to you, to explain myself." Natasha's voice shook. "To tell you what really happened that night with Paige."

Zoe bit her lip. The pain in Natasha's voice pierced her deep.

"So?" Natasha said. "Can we talk?"

"Sure," Zoe replied. "Come in."

25
NATASHA

Natasha stood by as Zoe fumbled with her keys. She'd barely said a word to Natasha, but she was willing to talk, and that was all that mattered.

She'd had several days to think about what to tell Zoe, but she still felt nervous. The morning after she'd gone to Zoe's sister's apartment, she'd woken up, called in sick to work, and stayed in bed all day. It was entirely unlike her. But she just couldn't face the world knowing that Zoe was gone from hers.

Once Natasha started to think clearly again, she realized she couldn't let things between the two of them end this way, so she'd packed her bags and gotten on the next flight to London. And here she was.

She didn't even care if Zoe forgave her or not. She just needed Zoe to know the truth. About that night. About why she had lied.

About what she felt for Zoe.

Zoe finally unlocked the door. They entered her apartment and sat down in the living room. Natasha glanced around. It looked a lot more like Zoe's home than her sister's apartment had. It was warm, bright and cozy, with cushions and throw rugs scattered haphazardly around.

Natasha looked at Zoe. She sat there, staring back at her, expressionless. Somehow, seeing Zoe like this hurt even more than being yelled at by her in the hall in the academy. Zoe wore her heart on her sleeve, and right now, she just seemed so numb. It was how Natasha knew how badly she'd screwed up. She needed to make this right.

They spoke at the same time.

"I should start—"

"How did you find—"

Silence hung in the air. Zoe fidgeted with one of her curls.

"You first," Natasha said.

"How did you find me?" Zoe asked.

"Dawn told me you went back to London."

"You talked to my sister?"

"I went to her apartment to see you, but she told me you were already gone. So, I came here. I had to do some detective work to find you. A friend of mine has a friend in the Royal London Ballet, so I asked her to find your address." Now that Natasha said it out loud, it seemed more than a little insane. "I know this is crazy. But I needed to see you. I need to explain myself."

"Okay," Zoe crossed her arms. "Go ahead."

"Where do I even start?" Natasha said. "I'm so sorry. For lying to you back then, and now, and all the time in between." She took in a breath, collecting herself. "It's true. I never got back together with Paige. Not that night, not ever. When I told you we were over long before you and I met, it was the truth. I should have told you all this sooner, but it's hard to talk about that night. There's more to it than you know." She hesitated. "What did Paige tell you?"

"She said she went to your place to pick up some things she'd left behind. And that she tried to mend your relationship, but you refused to get back together with her."

"That's one way to describe what happened. Paige's version of reality didn't always match up with everyone else's."

Zoe frowned. "What do you mean?"

"I never told you the whole truth about Paige, and why I ended things with her," Natasha said. "She'd always been an intense person. Not to mention jealous, possessive, irrational, sometimes manipulative. She had anger issues and mood swings. And over time, all those little cracks just got bigger and bigger. We'd fight sometimes, but since it never got physical, I never saw her instability as the red flag it should have been."

Natasha paused, waiting for a wave of unease to pass. She hadn't spoken about any of this in a long time.

"When I broke up with her, she had a hard time accepting it," she continued. "She kept asking me to take her back, to give her another chance. But eventually, she stopped, so I thought she'd finally moved on. It took some time, but I was able to move on too. When you and I started lessons together, I'd moved on completely. That's the truth.

"Everything was fine, until Paige and I started crossing paths again. It soon became obvious that she hadn't moved on. If anything, it was the opposite. Every time I saw her, she'd beg me to take her back. And each time, she seemed more and more disturbed. It scared me a little. I thought I was overreacting, but I should have trusted my instincts. I never thought she'd go as far as she did…"

"Natasha," Zoe said. "What did she do?"

"She snapped. Or, it might have just been quietly building and building over time, I don't know."

Zoe placed her hand on Natasha's arm. There was no anger left in her eyes. Just concern.

"That night," Natasha said. "Before you were due to leave for London, I'd just gotten home from work when Paige knocked on my door. I don't know if her timing was a coincidence. After everything that happened, I began to wonder if any of our encounters were really coincidences. Had she been watching me? Waiting for chances to run into me? Waiting for me to arrive home that evening? I usually didn't finish work that early. I only came home when I did because I didn't have a class with you.

"But I didn't suspect anything at the time. Especially because when Paige came to my door that night, she looked fine. Better than any of the other times I'd seen her. She was acting perfectly normal. It made me let my guard down. She had a box in her hand and said she wanted to grab some things she'd left behind at my house. I was wary, but she talked me into letting her in. She gathered her things, making small talk while she did so. But soon, the conversation turned. To us, our relationship. Paige apologized for everything she'd done. Then those apologies turned into promises to never hurt me again. Then she told me she needed me, and she had to have me back. I told her we were over for good. Then things got ugly."

"Ugly, how?" Zoe asked.

"I'll spare you the details. But Paige refused to take no

for an answer. She refused to leave, or to let me leave. When I tried, she would grab me or block the door. And she got angry. Angrier than I'd ever seen her. The way she was behaving was so erratic. She said she had to make me hers again. She started making all kinds of threats about what she'd do if I didn't get back with her. I told her she needed help. That made her even angrier. She just kept asking me why I didn't want to be with her.

"And then, she asked me if there was someone else." Natasha's voice caught in her throat. "I said no, but Paige didn't believe me. She just kept asking me if there was another woman, over and over. I kept denying it. I had to. It was true that I wasn't seeing anyone else. But she was right about one thing. My heart belonged to another."

Natasha felt Zoe shift beside her, but she didn't dare meet her eyes. She was afraid of what she would see in them.

"I don't know if Paige figured it out, or if she was just so delusional and jealous that she thought there had to be someone else, but she said she knew I was lying," she said. "And then she started making threats again. But this time, she said she was going to find out who stole me from her and make them pay. Make sure they stayed away from me for good.

"And for the first time that night, I was truly terrified. Hurting me, or herself, was one thing. But threatening someone else? Threatening you? It wasn't something I could ignore. I knew what Paige was like. How spiteful, how vindictive she could be. And I knew all about her insecurities. If she found out who you were? An up-and-coming dancer, younger and more talented than her? Her jealousy would have driven her to extremes."

"What did you think she'd do?" Zoe asked.

"That she'd expose us," Natasha said. "Tell everyone about you and me, use it to try to ruin you and your career before it even started. She'd done something like that before, to another dancer. Spread rumors to ruin her reputation. She didn't admit it, but I figured it out. It was what made me realize Paige wasn't the girl I fell in love with anymore. But that wasn't what I feared the most. I was scared she'd hurt you. Really hurt you. Especially because of how she was acting that night. At one point, I took out my phone to try to call someone, and Paige grabbed it from me and threw it at the wall. It smashed to pieces."

"Oh my god, Natasha," Zoe said. "I had no idea about any of this. I didn't know she was like that."

"I didn't see it coming either, but I should have. By then, it was too late. I felt trapped. I couldn't risk her finding out there was something between us. It seemed like the best thing I could do was cooperate with her. So, I told her I was open to getting back together, that we could talk about it, just to stop her from doing anything crazy.

"It worked. It took a while, but she calmed down. I still didn't know what to do. Paige just had this way of getting into my head, of twisting things. I was sitting there with her, no idea how to get out of the situation, when someone knocked on the door. It was you."

Natasha looked at Zoe. "I knew what you were doing there, Zoe. I knew you came to tell me you loved me. But I couldn't let you do that. Not with Paige right there inside. I couldn't let her figure out that the 'someone else' was you. I had to get rid of you as quietly as possible. So, when you assumed that Paige and I had gotten back together, I let you believe it. You were right that it was intentional. I mislead you, and I'm so sorry. But I had to do it."

"Why didn't you tell me?" Zoe said. "When I came to your door, why didn't you say something? I could have helped you."

Natasha shook her head. "That wasn't an option. I couldn't risk you getting pulled into Paige's web. Even after you left, Paige was suspicious of you. A student, coming to visit me late at night? A hushed conversation between us? And at that point, she was in such an irrational state of mind that she would have been suspicious of anyone who showed up at my door.

"Somehow, I managed to convince her you weren't a threat. I pretended that there was nothing between you and me, that maybe Paige and I could be together again, if she'd just give me some time and space to think. She agreed, but then she said she'd stay at my place overnight, on the living room couch, while I thought about it. And she still wouldn't let me leave. She was so unreasonable that it seemed logical to her, holding me hostage until I did what she wanted."

"How did you get away?" Zoe asked.

"I waited until Paige fell asleep, then I sneaked into the living room and took her phone since mine was broken. I called the police and told them what was going on. I didn't dare try to leave. I wasn't thinking straight, and I was afraid of what would happen if she woke up and found me gone. The police showed up. Things got messy. But in the end, they arrested Paige and took her away.

"I never saw her again after that night. I blocked her on

everything, and I was prepared to do more than that if she tried to contact me again. There was an investigation, but the case wasn't strong enough, so the charges were dropped. I have no idea what happened to her after that. I don't know if she got the help she needed. I heard from friends that she'd moved back to our hometown to live with her family. But I guess she came back to the city at some point."

"Natasha." Zoe's eyes were filled with pain. "I didn't know. I'm sorry you had to go through all that."

"It's all right," Natasha said. "It was a lifetime ago. I haven't even thought about it in years."

"I can't believe all that was happening, and I didn't see it. I was just so upset that night. I didn't realize anything was wrong. I'm so sorry."

"You had no way of knowing. And I made sure you were kept in the dark."

"I wish you'd told me the truth about what happened," Zoe said. "If not that night, then sometime later. I was just a phone call away. I would have understood. You were all alone. I could have been there for you."

"I couldn't burden you with something like that," Natasha said. "And I felt guilty about how badly I'd hurt you. I broke your heart. I didn't think you'd ever forgive me."

"Well, sure, I was heartbroken at first. But I wasn't mad at you. I knew that there was something going on with you and Paige that I didn't understand. It never occurred to me that it was anything so awful."

"It took me a long time to come to terms with everything. And after I finally did, I thought about getting in touch with you. But after what I'd done to you, and all the time that had passed, I thought the best thing to do was to let things be. I didn't want the pain of everything that had passed between us to get in the way of your new life. I thought that leaving the link between us severed was the safest way to do that. That way you'd be able to get over me and move on."

"I understand why we could never be together back then," Zoe said. "But I never got over you. How could I? You were the one who set me on the path to realizing my dream. You were the one thing that kept me focused enough to become the dancer that I became. You were my guiding star." She gathered Natasha's hands in her lap. "And for the past ten years, it was you who was on my mind whenever I took the stage. It was you who I was dancing for every single time."

"Oh, Zoe," Natasha said. "I've never told anyone this, but the truth is, I fell in love with you ten years ago. Even though I never let myself admit it, I did." She reached up to touch Zoe's cheek. "And now, I've fallen in love with you all over again."

"You know I loved you back then, Natasha. And I never stopped loving you." A gentle smile spread on Zoe's face. "I love you. I always have. I always will."

Natasha leaned in to kiss her. Zoe's lips dissolved into hers. Never in Natasha's life had she been more certain that this was exactly where she was supposed to be.

Zoe broke away, groaning. "I've really screwed things up, haven't I? Moving back to London? Now we're going to have a whole world between us again."

"We can make it work," Natasha said. "And I don't plan to be apart from you ever again."

"But, I have a job here, one that I think I'm going to love. I have a life here." Zoe sighed. "But none of that matters if I don't have you too."

"I didn't come here to take you back to the States with me, Zoe. I came here because I want to be with you no matter what. If that means moving to London, that's what I'll do."

"I could never ask you to do that," Zoe said. "You have a life and a job over there too. You can't just leave all that behind."

"I was getting tired of that life anyway. I'm ready to start a new one with you." Natasha paused. "That is, if that's what you want."

"Of course," Zoe said. "It's what I want more than anything."

26

ZOE

An hour or two later, they returned to Zoe's house after getting dinner at her favorite restaurant down the street. Zoe collapsed on the couch, Natasha next to her. It was still evening, but after the eventful day she'd just had, it felt much later.

"So," Zoe said. "What now?"

Natasha yawned. "Jet lag is setting in for me. I'm just about ready to go to bed, but it's too early."

Zoe shuffled closer to her. "I know how we can kill some time."

She drew a hand up the side of Natasha's face and kissed her. Natasha leaned into her, her lips dancing on Zoe's in that slow but insistent way that made her burn.

"God, I've missed this," Zoe whispered, her fingers curling through Natasha's hair.

"Me too," Natasha said. "It hasn't been long, but it felt like an eternity."

Zoe wrapped her hands around the nape of Natasha's neck, pulling her back in. Their lips touched with a crackle of electricity, sending sparks straight through to Zoe's core. Natasha pushed her back against the arm of the couch, pinning Zoe in place with her body.

Zoe quivered. Pushing Natasha away slightly, she snaked her hands down the other woman's front to yank her blouse out of her skirt. She slid her hands underneath it, gliding them up Natasha's bare stomach and grasping at her bra-covered breasts.

Natasha took in a sharp breath and pulled back, tearing her blouse off, then set to unbuttoning Zoe's shirt. Once she had it half open, she ripped it over Zoe's head. Her eyes rolled down Zoe's body, lingering on her bare chest. She dove down to kiss Zoe again, almost sending them tumbling off the couch.

"Now would be the perfect time to show me your bedroom," Natasha said.

Zoe grinned. "I have a better idea."

She tugged Natasha up from the couch, led her to a door in the hallway, and opened it wide, revealing a set of stairs descending under the house.

"Your basement?" Natasha raised an eyebrow. "I'm not sure I like where this is going."

"You will," Zoe said. "Just trust me."

She dragged Natasha down the stairs. When they reached the bottom, she flicked on the light, revealing a small dance studio, complete with a barre and mirrors.

"Isn't this amazing?" Zoe pulled Natasha over to the old wooden barre. "The house belongs to the company's old ballet master. She had her own studio built down here decades ago. She rented it out to me when she retired and moved away. I use it to practice."

"It's lovely," Natasha said. "But why exactly did you bring me down here?" Her face had taken on a no-nonsense expression, but the look in her eyes told Zoe that she already knew the answer.

"I was thinking about that night at the academy. After I helped you teach that lesson." Zoe hooked an arm around Natasha's waist. "I was hoping we could pick up where we left off upstairs."

"Were you now?"

"Don't pretend you didn't love it last time too."

"I did enjoy tying you up." Natasha spoke into Zoe's ear, her voice smooth as silk. "It's too bad I don't have anything to tie you up with this time, but I'll make do."

Natasha grabbed both sides of Zoe's face, kissing her hungrily. A thrill rolled up Zoe's spine. Natasha's hands wandered down Zoe's neck and chest, her palms skimming over Zoe's stomach. She unbuttoned Zoe's pants and pushed them down to the floor, then hooked her fingers into Zoe's panties. Zoe wriggled her hips so Natasha could work them off her legs, then she kicked them aside.

Natasha tutted. "So impatient."

Natasha spun Zoe around sharply to face the barre, pressing hard against her. Her breasts pushed into Zoe's back and her hot breath tickled Zoe's ear. Their eyes met in the mirror on the wall in front of them. A storm raged behind Natasha's. She wrapped her arms around Zoe, one over her shoulder and one hooked under her arm, and caressed her naked breasts.

Zoe squeezed her eyes shut and leaned back against her. Natasha planted searing kisses down the side of Zoe's neck and the back of her shoulder. At the same time, she slid a hand down the center of Zoe's stomach, all the way to where her lips met.

"You like it when I'm rough with you, don't you?" Natasha's finger crept into Zoe's slit, spreading her wetness along it. "What was it you said that first night at your apartment? That someone strict was exactly what you needed?"

Suddenly, Zoe felt a slap on her ass cheek. She gasped. Did Natasha really just spank her? It wasn't hard, but it was hard enough to make her skin tingle.

Another slap. She squealed with delight, a warm sensation spreading across her skin. That only seemed to spur Natasha on. Zoe opened her eyes to watch in the mirror. She found herself half bent against the barre, her ass stuck out behind her in a subconscious effort to get closer to Natasha's spanks. Blood rushed to her face, and right between her thighs.

"I was right." Natasha grabbed Zoe's ass cheeks in each hand, massaging them firmly. "You enjoyed that, didn't you?"

Zoe's answer was a blissful murmur.

Natasha drew her hand down between Zoe's cheeks, slipping it into her slit from behind. Zoe's mouth fell open in a silent moan. After running her fingers forward to tease Zoe's clit, Natasha pulled them back to her entrance. Slowly, she eased two fingers inside.

Zoe stiffened at the sudden jolt of pleasure. As Natasha delved in and out, Zoe's whole body turned to jelly. Gripping the barre before her, she rocked back into Natasha, watching in the mirror as they both lurched with every thrust. The old wooden barre creaked against her weight. She sucked in hard breaths. Natasha felt so good inside. The pressure deep within her intensified until she couldn't take any more—

Natasha withdrew. Zoe whimpered in protest.

"I want you to turn around, that's all," Natasha said. "I want to look at you."

Zoe turned to face her. Natasha gathered her into a heady kiss that sent the heat within her rising again. Zoe leaned back against the barre, half-sitting on it. Their lips still locked, Natasha ran her hand down between Zoe's thighs again. This time, she eased inside with no resistance at all.

"Oh!" Zoe gripped onto the barre behind her with one hand. The other, she slung around Natasha's neck, clinging on to her tightly, their cheeks pressing against each other. Her lips grazed the side of Natasha's face. Zoe could smell the sweet scent of her neck, could taste the salt of her skin, and could feel the heat radiating from her body. Natasha burned for her, just as much as Zoe burned for Natasha.

It didn't take long for Zoe to reach the edge again. As Natasha covered Zoe's lips with her own, pleasure burst inside her. She rose to her tiptoes, her weight on the barre, her head thrown back as an earth-shattering orgasm quaked through her.

Zoe's grip on Natasha slackened. She let out a deep, satisfied sigh, her body loosening. All the tension, the turmoil, and everything else she'd been feeling over the last few days had simply melted away. She felt light and free. Although she wasn't sure if she could stand up on her own.

"Do you need some time to recover?" Natasha asked. "Because I fully expect you to return the favor."

Suddenly, Zoe didn't feel tired anymore. "I'm good. And I fully intend to return the favor."

Zoe slung her arms over Natasha's shoulders, turning them both so Natasha had her back against the barre. She reached around and unclasped Natasha's bra, freeing her plump, perfect breasts. Zoe took one in her mouth, sucking and teasing a pebbled nipple. Natasha's hand fell to the back of Zoe's head, her chest arching out. Zoe buried herself in Natasha's chest, worshiping her breasts with her lips.

Natasha trembled. Zoe began kissing her way down the flat of Natasha's stomach in a long, meandering line. Pausing at the dip of her bellybutton, she unzipped the back of Natasha's skirt and pulled it down an inch, along with the top of her panties, then painted the curves of Natasha's hipbones with her lips.

Natasha's breath hitched. Sliding her hands down Natasha's sides, Zoe dropped to her knees and pushed the other woman's skirt up over her shapely hips. Natasha took the skirt from her, holding it up around her waist, allowing Zoe to strip her panties from her legs.

Zoe leaned in, taking in the scent of her arousal. She traced her fingers up the insides of Natasha's thighs, then ran them over the outside of her pale lower lips. Zoe let her lips brush against them gently.

A breathy growl emerged from Natasha's chest. She leaned down and took Zoe's chin in her fingers, tilting her up to face her. "Zoe, don't torment me any longer."

Zoe's lips curled into a smile. "Yes, ma'am."

She dove between Natasha's legs again and swept her tongue up Natasha's slit in one long, slow stroke. Above her, Natasha murmured feverishly. Zoe licked every inch of

Natasha's folds, savoring her taste. Then she settled her lips at Natasha's swollen nub, swirling her tongue around it.

Natasha shuddered. "Oh, yes!"

Overcome, she released the skirt she was holding around her waist. It fell over Zoe's head, trapping her underneath it, making Natasha's heat and fragrance even more intense. Drunk on the scent of her, Zoe licked and twirled her tongue, slow then fast, soft then firm, in every way she could. When Natasha began to shake, Zoe repeated that magic combination, over and over.

Moments later, Natasha's thighs clenched around Zoe's head, a cry rising from her lips as wetness spilled into Zoe's mouth.

Once her tremors subsided, Natasha drew Zoe up, kissing her lazily.

"Whew." Zoe clung onto her, barely able to stand. "I think I'm ready to show you my bedroom now."

"God, yes," Natasha said. "I want to go to sleep for a million years."

"That sounds perfect." Zoe smiled. "You do remember what you said last time, don't you?"

"I do." Natasha took Zoe's hand and pulled her toward the stairs. "This time, I promise I'll be there when you wake up. I'm not going anywhere. And I'm never going to let you slip through my fingers again."

EPILOGUE

NATASHA

*N*atasha took a seat in the front row of the theater. It was small, seating only a few hundred people, but every chair was occupied. The show was a step down from the big classical ballets Natasha was used to, and she'd already seen it three times, but she still found the experience magical. Although, that might have had something to do with the fact that her girlfriend was the star of the show.

It had been two years since Zoe stepped down as a principal dancer in the Royal London Ballet. But Zoe hadn't given up on dancing altogether. She hadn't been able to. Instead, she'd joined a small, local ballet company that focused on modern dance. They only held performances now and then, but that worked out well for Zoe. She still had a day job with the Royal London Ballet. This was her passion project.

The lights dimmed. Natasha sat up straight, eyes fixed on the stage. The curtain rose. A solitary figure crouched in the center of the stage, dressed in all black, her curls cascading loosely over her shoulders. As the music rose, so did Zoe.

Natasha watched her, transfixed. She would never tire of seeing Zoe dance. She moved with the same delicate beauty that she always had, but now she possessed this unshakable strength that spoke of a woman who had found herself in a world she'd once felt she didn't belong in.

Zoe was soon joined on stage by the other cast members, but Zoe outshone them all. This modern style suited her. She was freer. Wilder. It was a joy to watch. Zoe had told Natasha, again and again, that it was still Natasha she thought of when she danced. It filled her with warmth, knowing that all this was for her.

An hour later, the show ended to rapturous applause. Natasha filed out into the foyer with the rest of the crowd, then slipped backstage. Zoe spotted her and hurried over.

Natasha seized her girlfriend by the waist. "You were wonderful up there."

"You always say that," Zoe said.

"Because it's always true."

Zoe planted a kiss on Natasha's lips, then wriggled from her grasp. "I should help everyone pack up. Hopefully it won't take too long."

"I'll give you a hand," Natasha said.

By the time they were finished, it was past 11 p.m.

"I know it's late," Zoe said. "But tonight wouldn't be complete without one thing."

Natasha had been hoping Zoe would say that. She was feeling sentimental. And tonight was special, although she didn't think Zoe remembered what the occasion was. "The usual place, then?"

"Sure."

They left the building and headed down the street in the direction of a nearby ice cream parlor. Natasha had discovered the little shop by the Thames soon after arriving in the city. Since then, she and Zoe had made a comfortable life for themselves in London. They'd even bought the little terrace house Zoe had been renting, with the studio in the basement.

It had taken a while, but now, London felt like home to her. She and Zoe visited the States regularly, mostly to see their families. Natasha's father's cancer treatment had gone better than expected, and he still had a year or two ahead of him. Natasha was grateful. It had given her a chance to get to know her parents again.

They reached the ice cream parlor. It was about to close for the night, so they bought two ice cream cones and continued down the street. The path they followed ran alongside the river, a chill breeze blowing down it. A full moon hid behind the clouds.

Zoe shivered and slid her arm into Natasha's, huddling close to her.

"You know, we don't have to get ice cream every time you have a show when it's the middle of winter," Natasha said.

"I know." Zoe's breath froze as it left her mouth. "But I like doing this. It's our tradition."

"We could get something else instead. A hot drink, maybe?"

"It wouldn't be the same." Zoe let out a deep sigh. "Isn't this the perfect night? We probably shouldn't stay out too late, though. I have a lesson in the morning." It hadn't taken long for Zoe to realize how much she enjoyed teaching. She'd taken on a few private students of her own, who she taught in their basement studio.

"I won't keep you up for too long, then. I wouldn't want to get in the way of you molding impressionable young minds."

Zoe scrunched up her face. "When you put it that way, you make me sound like some crusty old schoolteacher."

"That's definitely not you. Your students love you. You're much better at the job than I ever was."

"Well, you taught me, and I turned out okay."

"Just okay?" Natasha said. "If you ask me, you turned out pretty well."

Zoe rested her head on Natasha's shoulder. "Don't you ever miss teaching?"

Natasha shook her head. "Not at all. As much as I used to enjoy it, choreography is a lot more interesting." After she left the academy, Natasha had realized that she wanted to try something more creative. She didn't regret it at all.

They continued down the path, strolling seemingly aimlessly. They should have been heading for home, but the night was too beautiful. And although she had only decided on it moments ago, Natasha was waiting for something.

A minute later, chimes sounded in the distance. She looked across the river and up at Big Ben. "It's midnight. Do you know what today is?"

A look of mild panic crossed Zoe's face. "Didn't we have our anniversary already?"

"I'm not talking about our anniversary. But it is a kind of anniversary."

Zoe thought for a moment, then smiled. "It's the day you came to London."

"That's right. It's the day I promised you that I was never going to let you slip through my fingers again." She reached into her pocket. "I wasn't planning on doing this tonight. I was going to do something big and dramatic. But this just feels right."

"What are you talking about?" Zoe said slowly. "Doing what?"

Natasha pulled the tiny, velvet-covered box from her coat pocket and opened it up before Zoe. "Showing you how serious I am about that promise I made you."

Zoe stared at the ring in the box, her eyes widening. "Are you asking what I think you're asking?"

"It's been long enough now, don't you think?" Natasha took Zoe's hand. "Zoe Waters, will you marry me?"

Zoe's mouth fell open slightly. "I…" She brought her hand up to her chest. "Yes. Yes, of course I will."

Her heart soaring, Natasha took the ring and slipped it onto Zoe's finger. It was a perfect fit. She pulled Zoe into an embrace and kissed her. The warmth of her body was more than enough to ward off the cold.

Across the river, Big Ben chimed for a twelfth time before falling silent.

Natasha took Zoe's hand. "Let's go home."

ABOUT THE AUTHOR

Anna Stone is the bestselling author of Being Hers. Her lesbian romance novels are sweet, passionate, and sizzle with heat. When she isn't writing, Anna can usually be found relaxing on the beach with a book.
Anna currently lives on the sunny east coast of Australia.

Visit www.annastoneauthor.com for information on her books and to sign up for her newsletter.

facebook.com/AnnaStoneRomance
twitter.com/AnnaStoneAuthor

Printed in Great Britain
by Amazon